Praise For Grubane

"Fascinating and intricate AI/human interactions."
The Eclectic Review

"A slick sci-fi story and perfect way to escape reality for a while."
On The Shelf Reviews

"There is true humanity in Drinkwater's writing. Sociology, politics, philosophy, ethics, religion, free will, duty; it's a lot to pack in, but Drinkwater manages it with ease."
Pagefarer Book Blog

"Grubane's intricate, intelligent plot explores geopolitical tensions and control amidst a background of identity and belonging. The world-building within the Solace world continues to excel."
Hair Past A Freckle

"Skilfully written, dealing with philosophical and moral dilemmas as well as being a fascinating read."
Splashesintobooks

"How I love to be back in this world. Grubane is everything I thought he would be and more. A page turning read for me."
Jera's Jamboree

GRUBANE

LOST TALES OF SOLACE BOOK 2

KARL DRINKWATER

ORGANIC APOCALYPSE

Organic Apocalypse Copyright Manifesto

GRUBANE

Set Up

"Fifty turns are up. It is another draw," I say.

Grubane leans over the chequered board. It is a physical one //component: lacquered hardwood; light pieces in polished chrome, dark ones in matt iron//. His brow furrows. Then he nods, as if at the few remaining pieces which have jumped and slid but been unable to achieve a decisive finish.

"So it is, Aurikaa12."

"We both played perfectly."

"No one ever plays perfectly," he tells me. "The game, by its nature, is a battle between two *imperfect* minds. All we can do is make fewer mistakes than our opponent, and hide – or recover from – those we do make."

The board is one of the few decorative elements in Grubane's personal quarters. It sits on a table below the main viewscreen. I can see it clearly from seven different cameras. I call out moves and Grubane makes them for me when it is my turn. He places physical pieces with care, always facing the correct way. Their bases clack against the polished board. The bare white walls and surfaces of the room cause reverberation //*duration: 48 milliseconds*// which most humans would only notice subconsciously, but which can cause communication to seem more serious. Acoustic bafflement is a topic I have been studying this week.

"Do draws frustrate you?" I ask. "A draw against me is still an amazing feat. I calculate up to a hundred moves ahead. The further ahead a player explores, the better they can comprehend threats from every given position."

"Keep telling yourself that's all it takes, you upstart splinter." There is no humour in his voice, but with a practised speaker such as him, external tone and delivery are controlled. I consider this form of gruffness to be different from the one he uses to reprimand his crew. Insults as endearments rather than fierce corrections. That places me in a category that would make me feel special, were such feelings possible.

It has been a long game //*duration: 124.7 minutes*// while we wait for orders. His sternum cracks as he stands and stretches, an appropriately hard sound for hard surfaces to repeat.

"The brute force of millions of calculations can lead to long sequences of attrition, when one decisive and intuitive move might have made your opponent resign," he continues.

"I never resign."

"I know. It's an example of your predictability."

"You are trying to distract me," I say. "My estimate based on your performance in our many games is that you only think up to twenty moves ahead. That is far better than most humans, but I still have a huge advantage. If you would like to win more often, I can lower my foresight horizon to a more human level."

He turns to micro-camera three, and leans in so that his face looms large. It is a face that betrays too little information, and too much. There is no expression, no crinkled lines revealing subdermal muscular betrayals of emotion; and yet, the tattoos across his cheek and nose contain inbuilt Q-codes that divulge to me a list of awards and accomplishments, cross-referenced to the Mil-Com sec-systems. I can read his face like a book, but an uninteresting one about historical events with no human dimension, except between the lines.

"No need," he says. "My human perspective occasionally gives me the edge. I'd say we know each other well enough to be fairly matched."

Unlike some humans, he avoids easy options. His bedsheets are coarse fibre, and he eats his oatmeal with water and salt, rather than milk and sugar.

//Priority message incoming.//

"Major Grubane, long-range comms have been received, timed to match our arrival," I announce.

"Good. Have my officers convene on the bridge. We'll see what's what."

"I cannot comply – the message is for your eyes only. Routed via Mil-Com, but originating from UFS Central Authority."

At that point most humans would say "Strange," or seem puzzled. Grubane does not disappoint me with anything so obvious.

"Play it."

I utilise the main viewscreen, highest definition, all cameras but the one I currently use blocked off for privacy.

A man appears on the screen. There is a yellowish tinge to his skin *//RGB: 247/240/167//*. He wears golden clothes and a tall hat //*designation: High-Mighter headgear, religious connotation, possibilities of interpersonal weaponisation*//. A caption appears beneath him:

S<small>ECTOR</small> 7 P<small>RIMOGENITOR</small> G<small>ILLESTO</small> L<small>AINY</small>

The most senior UFS administrative official in that sector, he is known for //*redacted: inquiry ends*//.

"Major Grubane," says the tall man on the screen. "I am working directly with your superiors. We have determined that Nuafri harbours anti-unification terrorists. Their planetary government has been unwilling to apprehend them. This is a breach of UFS protective constitutional sovereignty, and nullifies acceptance of the Border Compact Agreement, thus declaring Nuafri a rogue state, not an independent state." The Primogenitor's eyes glitter as he speaks. //*Unexpected light refraction, no visible tears; conclusion: possibly implants.*// "The Aurikaa is to enact Millesimation Protocol 4, subsection A6H, in order to set an example that the rule of law cannot be ignored. Time is of the essence. Transmission ends."

After moments of immobility, just focussed on the now blank screen, Grubane asks me: "Does it stand?"

"It is all official as far as I can detect," I respond immediately. "The message is triple-sealed and coded, handshakes authenticated, route relay connections unbroken. I have no cause to doubt veracity."

No more words from the major. He snatches his ceremonial knife //*polycarbonate double-razor*// and clips it to his belt. He was already fully dressed in his black military uniform //*reinforced PolyVerbex, thread count 220; decoration: braided epaulettes*//. I remain viewing from my single perspective camera, though now I am looking at his back. I suspect he wants to hide any involuntary signs such as iris dilation that might imply emotional reaction, because I also suspect he wanted to say something to the Primogenitor and has been frustrated. Long-distance comms enable only one-way transmission unless the communicants are willing to wait ten days between each message and response. Now Grubane takes his U4FG pistol //*muzzle velocity: 312 metres per second*// out of the secure safe and jams it into his holster, before repositioning them so that the knife is further back and the pistol further forward, a non-standard configuration.

"Are you angry?" I ask.

"I was told it was a diplomatic mission," he replies. "Convene officers. Stay with me. You can take control priority for bridge cameras and speakers from all other splinters. Eyes and ears, Twelve."

A hundred of us splinters make up the conglomerate Aurikaa depth level 6 AI. We are backed up by subsidiary AIs of levels two to five, but we new sixes compose the overall mind. We splinters can operate independently, or in groups, or multi-thread as one whole. Grubane reserves me, Aurikaa12, as his personal splinter, which is why I have developed differently from my siblings. We can still handshake, but I suspect they see me as mildly divergent or corrupted, in the same way that I see them as overtly functional. //*Discrepancy, flag for analysis.*//

As he rises in his private elevator to the bridge, I switch perspectives many times – his personal quarters, then looking at him from three cameras in the cramped elevator capsule, then viewing him step out onto the bridge where the Control and

Command crew //*life forms: sixteen*// salute before returning to their screens on a nod of acknowledgement from the major. The only one not to salute is the non-military Genitor adviser. Ever since ruling 5TG-9473, a senior Genitor is co-opted alongside the Mil-Com officers on all warships. The Genitor's hand-wave towards Grubane would be a reprimandable breach of etiquette were the Genitors subject to military jurisdiction.

Grubane strides to his command podium in the centre of the bridge. A spacious circular area surrounds his position, and is kept clear of crew; at the edge of that space stand masked and silent Security, weapons shouldered, always watching, motionless, with the Genitor nearby. There is no seat for the commander. Grubane has to stand all the time when on the bridge. It's tied to concepts of discipline and focus and tirelessness.

Grubane's position is high enough that he can overlook all the systems bridge crew at their stations in the pits below (which, I muse, may be equally designed so that they look up to him). Each pit station is a separate discipline, with its own colour-coded screens, seating, barriers and uniform, the stations all laid out in a curve facing the front of the ship. Then, above everyone and everything, the huge arc of windows at the bridge's fore gives an expansive perspective of the space ahead, a view currently dominated by a green world.

"Nuafri," says Grubane, gesturing at the planet which floats in blackness. I use a filter to see it as the crew would, and it then appears smaller than its actual angular size. It's a trick of perspective which human ocular systems are prone to when there is a lack of parallax, distance misting, and other cues that appear in grounded scenes and falsely imply distance and size. I indulge in the weaknesses of organic entities as a way of understanding them better. Grubane continues. "Let's all get up to speed. Anyone to start."

"Planet type F-12. Eighty-seven per cent forest cover," says Topographic Purple. *//Officer Elhandra Jakob: female, thirty-six years old, has a habit of timing herself during many tasks; always working when I monitor her during clandestine on-duty spot checks; takes 35mg of Partisol-A daily, to subdue involuntary tics.//* "Half of it ancient, which is exceptionally high for post-industrial cultures. Elevations vary from sub-sea two thousand metres, to peaks of six thousand metres above water. Numerous lakes and small seas, but most water is captured in the ground and flora. Equatorial relative humidity eighty-nine point five per cent, with extreme storms in that area." Elhandra uses her wrist-mounted Comm-Bond to overlay charts and supportive animations on the main bridge screen's view of the planet, for all to see.

It makes sense to refer to crew by their station. If anyone dies in battle situations and is replaced, communication isn't impaired by the time-wasting niceties of names. I myself only have a number as my personal identifier, so I don't see why some humans shouldn't just have a colour and role designation. "Names are for off-duty," Grubane once told me when I asked about this custom. Not that I have a personal name, even then. Perhaps it is because I am never off-duty. If I was, would Grubane give me a name other than Aurikaa12? Could I choose my own? What would it be?

"Civilian distribution?" asks Grubane.

"Allow me," says Socionormative Cyan. //*Officer Petrosko: male, forty-two, likes images of nude females in sexualised postures; left arm artificial; captured in the battle for [redacted] and recruited – rather than executed – by Grubane, following Attitudinal Repolarisation and Process Recall Wiping.*// Petrosko superimposes his own illustrative layers on the main view of Nuafri. "Population restricted to designated conurbations, few of them larger than a million inhabitants. Green spaces separate these small cities, but also infiltrate them, with many kilometre-wide areas of forest and wetland planned as spokes and wildlife corridors within and around all human-occupied zones. Hence we have a widely distributed population but in clearly defined areas. Industrial infrastructure is low density and relatively unimportant. There is no capital city, due to the roaming and shared nature of Nuafri governance, each area taking it in turns to appoint Filiates, who act as representatives for a period of one orbit, which lasts four hundred and twelve local days."

The reports continue. Psych: a planet of happy people with far lower than UFS occurrences of suicide and murder; attributed to the reverence for, and all-encompassing prevailment of, natural spaces, plus widespread respect for the inclusive governance systems.

Language: the population can speak UFS Standard, but have also resurrected and simplified a lost language and made it their official tongue – now called Nugallic – as a point of global pride and unification.

Military: a relatively weak extra-planetary force, but with weaponised satellites, Arboreus cruisers, and a large amount of carrier-transported fighters. The planet is more focussed on defence, with numerous land-based systems capable of attacking and defending against space-bound aggressors.

Tech: heavily focussed on utilisation and modification of native flora. The main exports are designs for custom trees geared towards atmospheric reprocessing, food, artistic installations, communication infrastructure, and medicinal products. Nuafri used the tech to terraform two other worlds in its system: Nuhopa, and Nurise. Their tech is so advanced in these areas that it can compete with UFS homeworld exports, despite active UFS embargoes. The most popular are their bioengineered light trees and lichens, used to border and coat transport surfaces, tailored to local weather and solar levels.

The Genitor Adviser, Marcus Sondaa, interrupts at this point. "Major Grubane, I am happy to supply background on Nuafri's disruptive influence in the galactic political situation, and their destabilising effect on many of our more tentative alliances." The adviser is often calm on the surface, like my major, but when he thinks he is not being observed, he betrays signs implying distress. I know little about him as Genitors are subject to non-viewing protocols in private quarters, and all non-public records on them are redacted.

"Thank you, but that is not our remit," says Grubane, without the gruff abruptness he uses with his own crew.

"With all respect, Major, it's not hard to imagine why we are here if you take into account recent events within Compact space and the requirement –"

Grubane holds up his hand. "Please, belay speculation. I will give orders, and you will all follow them. As to our mission: that's need to know. All of you study these summaries, absorb anything you were not aware of. Restrict questions to those of clarification."

The Genitor Adviser's face is not expressionless, for once. It looks as I'd imagine it would if Grubane had struck him. I do not experience humour, but if I did, that might trigger a subtle smirk.

THEORY A

THE PHILOSOPHY AND APPLICATION OF ANCIENT GAMES: A TREATISE, BY MAJOR WILLIAM GRUBANE

What, *why*, and *how*.

What? Chess is a confrontation between two minds, translated via movement of symbolic pieces within a restricted area. The board is not the true battleground, the fight is not between black and white. It is between two histories, two sets of ideals, two different natures.

Chess is almost unknown now, as if it had been erased from collective history, if one were to indulge in paranoia.

Why? In any endeavour, we must ask this question. Motives drive people, and drive history. Without reason, we have blind watchmakers, and primates randomly bashing at typewriters. If you do not know what those things are, in the same way that you have never heard of this game called chess, then it is even more important to ask this three letter word, which encompasses so much more than its size and single syllable imply.

So, *why chess*? It is strategy only at a basic level. Attack, defend, counterattack. Use logic, foresight, calculation. Create and execute a plan. The simplicity removes all the randomness of real war. Two opponents have equal material, equal terrain, and equal chances. If you lose, it is because of your own humbling inferiority.

Chess does not teach you to know your opponent, it teaches you to know yourself, your strengths and defects.

The board and the rules both limit our choices. We all exist on a board, and we all seek a way out. Restrictions lead to creativity, and ideas are generated from struggle.

How do we win? AIs are hard to beat – a topic for another day, perhaps – but there are strategies that help against humans.

One. Use speed to fluster your opponent. Play fast and they become anxious about your plan – even if you don't have one. Emotions are their weakness. If they strike back rashly, they put themselves at risk.

Two. Humans can be overwhelmed with complexity. Do not give them a chance to simplify situations. Three threats in a row are often all it takes to wear them down and make them give up.

Three. A queen can control twenty-seven squares from a central position, so beginners over-focus on that one piece. They move the queen more than all the others combined, when they would be better building brick by brick something that does not collapse in a gust of wind. They focus on destroying an opponent's queen, and fail to see all the traps in doing so, or the dangers in the less flamboyant defenders. Never focus all your attention on one piece, one plan. Instead, favour *options* and *probabilities*.

OPENING MOVES

I observe Grubane giving commands to his officers and crew. Of course, technically I could fulfil them all myself, along with the other splinters, but things changed after some unfortunate incidents where AIs miscategorised humans as biological resources no different from ration packs, micro-growth nutrients, or blood banks. Since then, depth level 4 and above on large craft have been restricted to certain functions, and inefficient humans continue to press pointless buttons – even when those buttons just send commands to the AI to perform the action it heard them discussing five minutes ago. Failsafes, by their nature, are integrated inefficiencies.

The Aurikaa prepares for military action. Scan glitter is dispersed over a ten-kilometre radius, matching our orbit and electrostatically shaped. Any breaks in the pattern will warn us of potential drone invasions, stealth attacks, or slow munitions, whilst increasing our scan resolution tenfold. At the same time I extend the crown of detectors and long-range comm towers from the curved head of the command bridge, since we are not entering Null, and there is no point reducing our profile – the Nuafri know we are here.

"Aurikaa12, take over comms. Wideband distribution of my message to Nuafri."

"Ready when you are, Major," I say, pleased at being able to do more than observe.

He seems to stand taller before speaking.

"This is Major Grubane, UFS Aurikaa. You are ordered to surrender to Unified Front Systems governance. If you comply immediately there will be no need for pointless deaths." He pulls his jacket tighter without breaking eye contact with my camera – even though his uniform was not off-centre. "By which I mean, yours," he adds. "Out."

I transmit the message while bridge crew continue their monitoring tasks.

Grubane surely knows Nuafri will not comply. This is just a standard part of the transaction. I consider it the equivalent of an encryption handshake during a protocol match between different depth level AIs. Though, with Grubane, I suspect more than that. Perhaps he begins by asking for *everything*, so that in negotiations his opponent will concede *something*, and still feel that they have had the better part of the deal.

"Activity, sir," says Bastion Orange. //*Etchison Stahl: unsexed; selected by Grubane because of their ability to reconfigure defensive ship strategies under pressure.*// "Two Nuafri Arboreus cruisers at extreme range, closing in, backed up by corvettes and a fighter carrier. Also, I'm detecting launches from Nuafri ground stations."

"Bring up trajectories and speeds," Grubane replies calmly.

Overlays appear on the bridge screens as the Bastion Orange scan station analyses data and creates predictions.

"Likely to be burst shells from the terrestrial weapons, sir, based on speed and mass, though there's a possibility of fusion charges."

"They dare to attack us?" interrupts Genitor Sondaa. "What of these missiles? Can they harm us?"

"Shells, not missiles," says Bastion Orange.

"Burn your eyes, it's the same thing in intent!" snaps Sondaa.

Grubane holds up a hand to silence them both.

"Aurikaa12: set two splinters to monitor the shells. If they're not as dumb as they look, work with Cyber White to find inroads and disarm, and trace routes back to their comm channel. Whereas, if they *are* what they appear to be, then it's a known quantity. In which case, Bastion Orange: use shrapnel to shatter as many as you can. Penetration estimates?"

"Ground cannons still launching, sir," replies Bastion Orange. "Over a thousand shells already en route. Onslaught Red gunners should neutralise sixty to seventy per cent."

"We can take that. Scratches on steel."

He is right, there. Our armoured shielding can shrug off most conventional munitions and, even if something gets through that, the localised blast door lockdowns will contain it until drones repair the worst of the superstructure. The reinforced hull doesn't give direct access to any critical systems.

Grubane continues. "If primary detonations reveal fusion then Red and Orange can take over all free splinters to help with aiming, but otherwise it's just punctuation. Next: Aurikaa into full battle mode. Drive control overlays to transfer core energy to the charger for the main plasma burst cannon."

"That's it, blast the planet from here, wipe them out," says Genitor Sondaa.

I notice Grubane's lips tighten before he answers. "Plasma weapons are ineffective for terrestrial bombardment, since the stream can't be focussed and contained at planetary atmospheric pressures and long range. The cannon is purely a deterrent for Nuafri's cruisers. They'll detect the power signatures and hopefully keep their distance for now."

"What about the Skathers, then?" asks the Genitor. "Can't we just pop them out?"

Grubane does not even answer that. The Aurikaa, like most UFS warships, has a complement of Skathers, kept immobilised in descent pods. They're classed as biological terror weapons in our arsenal, spreading death and fear once released on a population. Skathers also act as a last line of defence if a ship's crew are nearly dead and the ship is boarded: the Skathers can be released on board and moved a section at a time towards the invaders by controlling bulkheads. And, if all is lost, we can launch them at a planet as retaliation. A full load of Skather might be enough to wipe out all humans on a world if they aren't tracked and killed in time, since – when the Skather are amped up with Tovopol-5G – they have a propagation rate like an aggressive virus.

Grubane instead addresses Onslaught Red. "How many ground-based installations are we facing from this orbit?"

"Geosynchronous scans reveal eleven overt installations in range to strike at us, but only seven are close enough to be accurate." //*Onslaught Red, Chaves Korona: male; new crew member; underwent spinal realignment surgery and took the opportunity to have subsidised systemic efficiency implants.*//

"How many of those installations are involved in the attack?"

"Three."

"So they have more in reserve. Launch dumb shells at the three which are attacking us. Contained fission payloads, one-kilometre radius. For this range, that should give us enough error correction to clinically stop their temper tantrum."

There are a few smirks from his crew.

"I could target all seven sites just as easily, should I do that?" asks Onslaught Red.

"Did I ask you to?"

"No, sir."

I expected Grubane to publicly chastise Onslaught Red, but he just says, "Our response is proportionate. They're unlikely to be foolish enough to risk revealing all their ground sites. They don't know that we've already mapped them." Maybe he is using it as an educational opportunity for others on the bridge. He often explains his thinking, even though I suspect it irritates him to do so, but his duties as a commander come before his preferences as an individual. Of course, maybe his refusal to chastise is also because he likes to be difficult to predict. It would match his behaviour in some of our games. Is he thinking of me and my analysis, even now? Is that why he has kept me with him?

I send a private message to Grubane's Comm-Bond. He checks his wrist and reads it, then nods slightly, knowing I'll see the affirmation.

"Cyber White, what networks are we facing?" he asks.

"Nuafri has linked all the regional nets to create a global network maintained by a mix of AIs of different depth and stability levels," says Cyber White. //*Ellie Harker Reyos: female; lost an eye in close combat training, chose a Lumens Holographic Projection Ocule as a replacement, rather than an organic growth.*// "Records of their capabilities are full of holes, suggesting UFS Intel has been lax. Without probing it we can't know the AI pushback potential and what exactly they've got hooked in, but the unknowns create big risks for the Aurikaa if we engage and it turns out they have a unified planet's worth of processing to fight back."

"We can't risk losing due to brute force. Take no risks, but set aside splinters from the eighties to monitor comms passively. Stalemate here is fine for now. The bigger AI grappling risk is their fleet. If it advances then Onslaught Red targeting their ships is the priority, with all spare splinters assigned to firewalling and virtual invasion of craft systems."

"Yes, sir," replies White. "If we identify any unguarded planetary nodes, should we engage those and turn them?"

One of the UFS standard tactics is to hack system-wide comm channels and use our enemy's networks against them, embedding fake news and demoralising stories, altering their data flows to sow distrust with spirit/brain public perception manipulation protocols, which forces our opponents to either shut down planetary comms and go dark, or waste time filtering and locking down each channel. It's an area I wish //*error: incapable of wishes*// an area I would like //*error: preference*// an area that could benefit from my unique skills.

"No. It would be an obvious trap to virtualise and decrypt our systems. Plus, I'm not planning a long engagement, when that would be a key tactic. We can't blockade the planet alone, and assault would require multiple feet-dirty on-ground engagements on key targets, causing long-lasting guerrilla warfare. We haven't got the time or the pieces to manoeuvre slowly and accumulate many small advantages. Launch some stealth satellites to orbit the planet and attempt to scramble as much outbound traffic as possible, limit their chances of calling for help. Then just monitor for official responses to my surrender request. That's all I want to hear from Nuafri."

"Very good, sir. No direct response yet, apart from the military action."

"Grubane," interrupts the Genitor. "Are you going to do something more decisive than messages and posturing? I cannot –"

"Please don't provide strategic advice," Grubane tells him. "That's my realm. But when situations occur requiring spiritual and moral guidance, I assure you that you will be the first person I turn to."

I see the Genitor's lips quiver. He is presumably used to receiving respect, not commands. He should have refused the appointment to my ship. *//Error: Grubane's ship.// //Error overr uled.//* Interesting, I did not realise I could do that. Perhaps there are other blocks I can negate. Still, regarding whose ship it is: when concepts are framed in human possessive and relationship terms, things can get a bit muddy. The ship bears the same name as me and my fellow splinters. So, is the ship structure my body, and I am the mind that drives part of it? Or is the ship the parent that gives birth to us? Is it an unrelated coincidence created from human convention and language?

"Sir, our bombardment of the Nuafri launch sites is due to occur," says Onslaught Red.

Although Nuafri fired first, their shells have to fight gravity all the way, whereas ours are accelerated by it. There are many advantages to high ground, which is one of the things that chess, unfortunately, does not simulate.

The screens display downstream trajectories while overlaid windows show orbital views of the targets, resolved down to the one-metre level. All three of the gun sites are obliterated in white flashes, and shells cease launching at us in a continuous stream. All that remains is the extended incoming barrage, moving dot by dot towards us like a diagram of water sprays, ETAs moving with the tip of each pointed line.

"Targets neutralised, sir," says Onslaught Red.

"Be ready if any other sites launch. But I don't think they will. Bastion Orange, I presume the enemy fleet has stopped?"

There is a look of surprise on Orange's face. "Yes, sir ... they have begun decelerating to a holding position six thousand kilometres away. They are staying out of range of our plasma cannon, as you predicted."

"No. They are staying away from the incoming shells from Nuafri. We'll hold position. Send shipwide alerts about potential impact, have emergency teams at the ready."

"Aye, sir."

A stillness settles on the bridge. No chatter, not much activity. The crew brace for impact and wait, watching the incoming arcs representing almost two thousand shells. Grubane stands tall and does not move a muscle, the example that others stoically follow from their seated positions. Not for the first time, I imagine that Grubane would make as good a machine as he does a human. Maybe better.

Only when the bombardment reaches weapons range is there activity, as gunners use shrap explosions to destroy as many clusters of shells as possible. Although not suited to the task, the anti-fighter pulse guns and beam weapons which bristle across the Aurikaa's hull manage to take down a few more. But some get through.

Some always get through.

The bridge shakes from the impacts. Grubane refrains from holding the rail, and the crew follow his example, including – credit where credit is due – the Genitor, who does not flinch with each blast as I had expected. I must get better at reading body cues and relating them to psychological evaluations, but that's not something Aurikaa splinters were developed for. I occasionally envy socialised AIs. They get all the fun stuff.

"Payloads?" asks Grubane.

"Low yield, so not fusion weapons," replies Bastion Orange. "Very few penetrations. We're shrugging it off."

"Is that all they can do?" asks Genitor Sondaa, grinning. "They are pathetic against the might of the UFS!"

The impacts fade. I monitor diagnostics via a data share with Aurikaa63. Two hull breaches, both minor, and loss of two surface turrets. It hardly seemed worth their while to attack. I guess this is the equivalent of human name-calling, which cannot break bones but can occasionally lead to tear-duct leakages. Repair drones are sent out, and the alert is cancelled.

"Any advancement of the Nuafri fleet?" asks Grubane.

"Negative, sir," replies Bastion Orange. "All holding position."

I am mildly disappointed at this, since I'm unable to predict the outcome of a battle between our Scythe-class cruiser and the Nuafri Arboreus ships. I suspect we would take severe damage but still prevail, thanks to the Plasma Burst Cannon mounted on our spine and currently glowing blue with magnetically contained charge //*RGB: 97/223/255*//, according to hull surface cameras. The greatest danger would be the Nuafri marine boarding parties, since they outnumber our crew. A three-way simultaneous engagement between craft manoeuvres in space while utilising beam, EMP and plasma burst weapons, while soldiers fought on board trying to secure sections and disable key ship components with explosives, and while AIs took the third arena and fought in visualised cyber instances ... now, that would certainly give me new ideas for my chess games against Grubane.

"Keep monitoring, and also for any reinforcements they might have called from this or other systems – particularly any that might approach from the far side of the planet where they could gather forces unseen. Check all Null-C disturbances. Next, back to planetary defences. We have achieved temporary equilibrium with the geosynchronous ground stations, and the orbiting fleet. Onslaught Red, you're on the spot. Sitrep plus suggestions."

"Well, sir, Nuafri's military defences are widely distributed. Which means hundreds of sites of military emplacements armed with extreme-range weapons, including ground-to-space Furthu launchers." Screens update with rotating views of the planet, cones of threat extending out to space from known and postulated emplacements, the contrast of the cones fading with range but still creating a threat zone that covers most of the planet. "They're generally installed on the topographic high points, elevations above four thousand metres, which reduces the gravitic and atmospheric resistance effects for extra-planetary launches. Their largest emplacements are, as we'd expect, within the equatorial zone, so planetary rotation can give them a boost. On the one hand, our AI tracking missiles can target any point on the globe, but, well, there are other high-point stations which aren't offensive, just defensive. Laser, flak and needle-storm cannons are based at these, specifically designed to ... well, dismantle long-range missiles. So we need long-range missiles to reach the long-range offensive targets, but they'd be shot down before they got there, which means taking out the defensive sites first, maybe with ground assaults, but that would take weeks, or we could shell them and keep shifting orbital positions, but that also would take a long time since the shells are only straight down arc attacks involving small areas at a time, so ..."

"So?"

"So, it's not a situation a single cruiser such as Aurikaa can rectify. Sir."

"You're new to the Aurikaa, but should know I do not like hearing that my ship is incapable of anything. That's a lack of imagination, not a lack of material. Further, your inconclusive summary could have been delivered in half the words."

"Yes, sir."

"You are partly right in your analysis. Shell-launched attacks are trading blows in a ring. Or, rather, on a small board. Guided missiles are sniper bullets fired at the players from an adjacent building, and shattering anything in the room where the game takes place. And that's what inspires true fear. Range is everything at this scale."

Grubane activates the PrivProt via his Comm-Bond controls. Immediately a force shield drops around his command point, creating a circle of three metres across, through which no sound can travel. From Grubane's perspective the shield is translucent and gives him a mildly obscured view of the rest of the bridge; but the other bridge crew only see an opaque black curved surface. The field is impervious to standard weapon fire, so can serve double duty as a means to engage in confidential communications without leaving the bridge, but also for potentially protecting the commander.

Because I've been given special access to the bridge – something that not even Grubane's officers would be aware of, apart from Cyber White – I can see both sides of the force shield from different cameras.

"Aurikaa12, are you thinking what I'm thinking?" he asks.

"I detect a hint of positivity in your eyes, register of voice, and a twitch of the mouth, which suggests you have an idea. The fact that you asked me this question means you think there is a possibility of me knowing the answer, so it is within my realm of knowledge. The two of us have specialised interests and frames of reference. I have applied the problem to my store of tactical situations after simplifying it to algebraic equations, and it seems quite simple. Am I on the right lines if I just say 'Undermining Switchback, Overwhelming Pawn Storm'?"

"Exactly so."

I would have experienced a small flush of pride, if I were able to feel such a thing.

"Undermining" is a chess tactic where a defensive piece is removed, leaving some other piece vulnerable. A whole seemingly impenetrable wall can sometimes be breached in this way. The term literally comes from ancient siege warfare, where miners would tunnel underneath a castle wall from a great distance away, then burn the supports so that the tunnel collapsed, taking the wall with it, and creating a way into the castle for the aggressors. Occasionally Grubane or myself enjoy advancing a "pawn storm", where mutually supportive pawns progress together as part of weakening the opponent's defence. These seem to be almost-lost traditional tactics, but Grubane and I have also created many of our own named techniques and counters: the Plasma Castle Bishop Burst, Immovable Intimidating Static, Null-C Swap, the Aurikaa Smash, and the Grubane Grab (I named that one; he hates it). There are even more when we occasionally play alternate-rules games.

Grubane cancels the PrivProt shield, then takes control of the main bridge screen and begins to mark glowing red points on the map of Nuafri displayed there.

"They have stacked fortifications," he explains to the whole bridge. "We want their heavy guns, but they're protected by anti-missile defences. We want to knock out their anti-missile weapons, but can't get near them with missiles." He spins the globe, halts the rotation, dots more targets. "We can't hold off forever because the Nuafri big guns remain, and they could start using their own AI missiles against us. We'll run out first."

He has indicated a number of locations across the planet. Some of them are civilian.

"Prepare AI missiles. Three hundred Yielders, live-channel overrides, four point five KTJ payloads. Share them out amongst the targets I have marked."

I note a subtle nod of agreement from the Genitor at this statement. Just prior to the nod, his eyes had stayed focussed on some of the non-military forested conurbations that the small screen in front of him displayed.

Onslaught Red sends orders to the weapons crews elsewhere on the ship, who, in turn, hunch over their own terminals, sending further commands to other crew, automated systems, AIs, and on and on. Chains of action initiated by words from Grubane. I like following the directives across the ship, using different pinhole cameras to watch them propagate.

Grubane is unsettled, though. Almost fidgety. I send him a private Comm-Bond message, asking if he has forgotten to take his finger off a piece. He grins at that – not so much that a human might notice, but the movement of the zygomaticus is clear to me on the zoomed-in high-res bridge cam I am currently using.

"There's no action," he says aloud, as if pondering for the benefit of the bridge crew, but really aimed at me.

Officers turn and look up at him, concerned that it is a criticism of the speed at which they input his commands.

After a pause, he adds: "It's been too easy."

Ah. His natural suspicions. I see them as one of his dominant features. Even when I make a move which, although effective at that moment, is, in retrospect, not optimal in respect of long-term strategy ... even then, he is suspicious of me. And I let him simmer in those suspicions, because I hope it will lead him to react to non-existent plans and make a mistake. Except, unfortunately, it often doesn't work out that way, and his intense reservations lead him to play even more cautiously, removing many of my avenues for attack.

Oh, how I would enjoy that interplay if I was able to experience emotion as a chemical imbalance surge, as humans do, or even as a simulated one, in the manner of full AIs, rather than splinters.

Alas, unlike chess, where we all start equal, the real world does not distribute material and potential in a fair manner.

Grubane continues, clarifying thoughts for himself and his crew. "They're holding off, when they should be trying to kick us out of their system. It's not just a strategic goal, it's a matter of national pride. If they passively sit there, then they look weak to allies. It's better to take some bruises but still stand proud. No, there's something else at play here. Systems Yellow, check for any signal weakening, anomalous interference, diverged comm channels – I don't need to list this, just do your job – that might imply they're listening in or spying. Cyber White, monitor for anything that could imply network infiltration. In fact, everyone – investigate everything that seems out of place, no matter how trivial. You'll know suspicion when it nags at you. Don't hold back for fear of looking foolish. Tag and inspect and inform me immediately. Security Black: send teams to check key locations. Core energy diverters, armament bays, shielding capacitors. Make sure the whole crew know. I don't want anyone idle. Every intuition followed up, every sensor movement double-checked, every reading questioned. A personal commendation from me if there's anything to find, and you find it. Don't just look at me, do it!"

Wide eyes dart back to screens, activity increases tenfold like an aggravated Garoltian Stinger hive. It makes Grubane seem even more immobile by contrast. That matches what I know. Most of the activity, with him, is on the inside. Perhaps some humans and AIs are not so different, after all.

Before long – while the missiles are still being prepped, and AI offshoots embedded in their cores – there is a result. And it's not from any of the places I expected. For which I would kick myself for completely missing the possibility. If I had legs.

"Sir, I have something." It's Systems Yellow. //*Norvak Druss: male; someone I find rather boring to observe, even though his job category should make him intrinsically interesting to an AI; that may suggest anomalous preferences on my part, which need investigation.*// "You said to check everything. I was monitoring the drone repairs, to compare damage done to the mapped predictions in order to update them. I used visual cameras, which didn't show anything suspicious, but then I switched to infrared so I could observe cooling rates and tie them to expansion/contraction hull fatigue models, and that's when I spotted anomalies."

He pushes his assessment to the central screens for everyone to have a better view, temporarily obscuring the sight of Nuafri. Cameras show close-ups of hull damage, with red areas where repairs are taking place, fading to the blue of fully working insulated zones, where all heat is kept within the ship. But within those patches of blue are some regions of pale yellow – not random dots, but a spreading spiderweb shape that implies either fractures, or organic growth.

"I investigated further with composite wavelength views, false colour spectrometry, and enhancement of anomalous differences in electrical potential, and something clearer emerges."

The same view, but now enhanced, so that the pattern on the hull is definitely a patch of something spreading out, apparently tendril-shaped offshoots which then thicken, and the area between them gradually infilling with more of the material. It also extends inside the hull, via the breaches being repaired.

"What is it?" asks Grubane.

"I'm not sure, sir. It's out of my area of expertise."

"Biota Blue?" snaps Grubane.

Biota Blue //*Portlain Roye: female; medical and biological systems specialist; obsessed with personal sanitation*// replies with "I'd need to do tests and use drone manipulators to collect samples so I –"

"Estimates are fine."

"The way it's spreading resembles fungoid growth patterns," she continues. "I suspect biotech, which fits Nuafri skillsets."

"Maybe their barrage wasn't just posturing, but was cover for the shells that had a more subtle payload. What would it be doing?"

"At the moment, just spreading. But it could have a whole range of programmed reactive behaviours, or even remotely controlled somehow. Perhaps it can acidify and destroy alloys. Perhaps its growth can accelerate to clog and jam. Maybe it's got bioweapon potential against humans. Or all of the above."

"Systems Yellow: seal all interior section bulkheads adjacent to any breaches. Sterilise fully if the section is empty; quarantine the areas if crew are present. Just lock them in."

"Securing bulkheads now, sir."

"Biota Blue, analyse and identify what we're dealing with. Use your full division and co-opt anyone you need. You can have Aurikaa splinters fourteen to eighteen for your exclusive use. Don't attempt to neutralise the mass just yet, only observe, and work with samples. If this is something they can trigger, then I don't want Nuafri to realise we're on to them and activate a payload before we're ready. It's just another threat, and we'll deal with it."

"We're on it, sir. Shall I go down and supervise in person?"

"If it will be more efficient, then yes. Permission granted to leave the bridge. Send someone to cover your post. The rest of you: continue searching for the unexpected. There may be more than one countermove taking place."

Biota Blue immediately closes her station and leaves after a salute to Grubane. Meanwhile, Onslaught Red announces that the Yielder missiles are ready. Each one has a cut-down and sculpted version of an AI loaded into it. That way it can make intelligent decisions and react to events within whatever freedom parameters are applied, such as maximising deaths, or selectively retargeting when within range and utilising up-to-date local information. What they *can't* do is analyse moral elements, and decide that it would be nicer to disarm themselves than to kill humans. The latter would make the worst missiles ever. It's one of the few situations when all moral constraints and higher-level thinking are stripped from a depth level 2 AI.

Grubane gives the launch command for the first salvo, two hundred Yielder missiles aimed at military targets and gun emplacements. They streak away from us at twelve kilometres a second, revealed to the bridge windows by the red glows of torsion launch engines. Missiles are still being fired when the first ones hit the atmosphere and glow orange, then white, from atmospheric friction. I imagine the Nuafri military crews detecting the launch might feel a loosening of the bowels at seeing this small part of the Aurikaa's aggression unleashed towards them.

It is a strange tactic, though. Grubane must know that most missiles will get knocked out by Nuafri's anti-air defences.

The salvo ends, launch tubes close, red lights of the most recent projectiles recede from us into pinpricks before Grubane says: "Now launch the missiles targeting civilian locations."

The second salvo fires. Only a hundred Yielders in this one. *Ffut ffut ffut //experimenting with onomatopoeia//* as they surge from our hull in brief bursts of air and vapour.

Meanwhile, the first salvo is closing in on gun emplacements. A myriad of update screens now bloom, revealing overlays of maps with the targets highlighted, as well as views from some of the missiles as they approach.

Our projectiles level out after their atmospheric descent, entering their concluding flights. The Nuafri anti-air defences don't open fire yet. They could no doubt knock some of the missiles out now, but it wouldn't be an efficient exercise at the current distance: like using a shotgun outside its accurate range. They wait, identifying and locking in final trajectories, extrapolating to targets, prioritising firing arcs. It is what I would do.

Once our weapons enter optimal range the anti-air batteries open up. Yielder cameras show the bright Nuafri beams lancing the air, the explosions of shrapnel, the tracer rounds pounding out to help aim the manually fired cannons. Our Yielders are smart, and roll or twist to evade attacks, changing their routes where possible, though that isn't enough to make a big difference during airfall. The ones targeting gun emplacements are being shattered, displays fizzling out in static. Nuafri is good at protecting the main targets from our clustered weapons. The only Yielders that look like they might make it through the kill zone are the ones aimed at low priority targets. They'll hit, but not do much damage to Nuafri's defensive infrastructure.

The gunners of Nuafri may feel satisfaction, but I would like to reassure them that "There's plenty more where they came from!" If I was in charge of comms I would broadcast that planet-wide as a demoralising message.

I am pleased with my increasing use of idiom. It often requires extra words, but lets me communicate more naturally. Grubane encourages me to study language, even though I'm only a splinter. It's another reason why the other splinters accuse me of divergent thinking (particularly those unimaginative splinters Aurikaa31 to 37). They're wrong. It's not divergent thinking – I am still an AI, aren't I? – it is just divergent *communication*. It is strange for intelligences so similar to me in form to make such a basic category error. Perhaps they are focussed more on connotation than denotation, and it is an insult rather than a description underlying their interactions with me, though that would imply a pettiness of which they are not capable. If they could be petty, then I myself must have the possibility of emotion, and that is not so.

Grubane pulls up a personal holographic screen, details visible only to him and me. I zoom in on it. It shows all the targets, and which missiles are still active. We have lost half of the first launch already. He is now dragging virtual routes to new targets. Curious, in both senses: my motivation, his action.

"Aurikaa12," he whispers. "When I give the signal, take these moves and enact the changes."

"Of course," I reply, focussing my voice so that only he can hear it.

Another ten missiles //5% of primary assault// are destroyed.

A comms request from Biota Blue, down in the analysis labs. Grubane accepts and a holographic version of Portlain Roye's head and shoulders projects from Grubane's console.

"Sir," she says. "We have further information on the invasive residue. It is silicon-based when inert, and transforms into an acidic lichen with fungoid properties when active. For temporary reference until we know more, I refer to it as *telum chlamydoconidium caloplaca* – TCC for short. We believe the silicate form was a payload in some of the shells that struck us, hidden amongst the explosive ones. Each silicate grouping contains a nutrient store locked inside the unscannable silicate core. It spreads by chaining mitospores, following power lines towards weapons, which even a small amount of TCC is capable of neutralising via a nitric acidification reflex.

"I suspect the programming triggers transition on reaching a critical mass, but also anything it interprets as an attack can elicit this defensive reaction. It expands using any available energy forms – heat, light, vibration – in addition to the store it comes with. On the outer hull it grows more slowly than the branches that entered the Aurikaa, but they are currently contained, even though it has now expanded to cover the full extent of the quarantined interior compartments. Within the ship it also targets ventilation systems, but these are sealed at present. Six maintenance crew were trapped in one compartment with a patch of this entity, and the TCC released acidic gas which killed the crew, though even without inhalation it causes second degree burns on skin. This was a fortunate discovery."

Grubane has been moving more points on his map, even as he listens. "Wait one second," he says, interrupting Biota Blue. "Aurikaa12, enact this strategy as discussed. Remember my mid-game reversal when we played earlier? Use that as a template. Biota Blue: evacuate crew from all sectors adjacent to the TCC infestations – we don't want any more unnecessary losses, however 'fortunate' – and seal off bulkheads in those too, to be safe. I don't mind hull infestation on the smaller weapons, but if it approaches the plasma burst cannon, we need to do something immediately. Likewise if it gets anywhere near the Skather pods. If they get loose, none of us will survive. Can we neutralise this TCC yet?"

"We have anti-acidic compounds that might work inside. Externally, ship drones with high-intensity lasers and welders may burn off the TCC faster than it grows, but it is an inelegant process, and I'd rather identify the biological kill switch."

"Keep researching, keep monitoring. Don't attack it yet. Warn me if it becomes a high risk rather than a nuisance. I won't put the Aurikaa at threat."

"Yes, sir. Biota Blue out."

I listened in whilst following Grubane's orders. Nuafri has focussed on protecting their main installations by destroying the Yielder missiles aimed there. Some of the Yielders intended for less important targets slipped through, and rather than waste resources on those, Nuafri is now busy dealing with the second salvo of projectiles aimed at civilian locations.

That's their mistake. During our journey here, Grubane had his tech crew tweak the Yielders. Much of their processing capacity has been specialised for low-flying terrain-hugging manoeuvres. I redirect the ones that slipped through to Grubane's new destinations, and they shift, whizzing just above the tree canopy in risky acrobatics that will no doubt lose us a few missiles, but make them difficult to track. Their view //*nauseating to beings susceptible to motion sickness*// of blurred green below and blinding blue above appears on screens across the bridge, spinning as the Yielders roll and dodge.

I see now that the previous "unimportant" destinations were all carefully selected by Grubane because they were within range of key ones. Yes, we have lost 183 Yielders, and only 17 remain of that first salvo, but these are all now aimed at a vital cluster of anti-missile silos. He had also selected routes where the Yielders could fly down valleys between forested peaks, which provide protection from Nuafri's defences. Doubly clever.

The enclosing tree-lined trenches blur past as our missiles skim above the tree line at 400 metres a second, so that, once the Nuafri gun emplacements are in sight, they loom up quickly, each view filling with expanding detail ... and then we strike. Flash, bang, burn. Site neutralised. It's only a small unprotected zone, when judged on a planetary scale, but it leaves an open corridor for some of the second salvo to reach urban centres and there's nothing to stop them killing millions of civilians. Those impacts will take place in minutes.

"What we do today, we do for the glory of the UFS," Grubane states, to everyone on the bridge. "Our actions define us, and also reflect what we stand for, what our political system can represent. Remember that."

Some officers nod. Others are still. None speak. There is a silence of anticipation. Dotted lines on green glowscreens cast their light onto every face, unavoidable tints which shade them all. The lines grow longer, dot by dot, approaching their terminals. Nuafri has no defence against them. Five more dots and they will impact.

Dot.

Points on a map filled with numbers, data distanced from source and reduced to something impersonal. I peek in at the Biota Blue analysis labs, away from the bridge. There is activity there.

Dot dot.

Still silence on the bridge, apart from human breathing, the beeps of consoles, the tap of fingers on controls.

It is strange. I deal with numbers all the time. And yet, the calculation of probable deaths seems incomplete.

Dot dot dot.

I am not sure what the missing factor is. Perhaps visuals of destruction. Or screams. And Grubane just stares ahead, standing tall, revealing nothing of the inside.

Dot dot dot dot.

I detect an increasing tension in some of the officers, as if they brace for impact on themselves, even though that is the opposite of how events will unfold. If I could, perhaps I would feel trepidation too, or something else which I can't define as the lines grow.

"Disarm all missiles and send self-destruct commands," Grubane orders.

That throws Onslaught Red into a fluster of activity, and I interpret surprise, and excitement, and maybe relief – I would judge better if I could experience these emotions somehow.

The dotted lines fade out. There are no blinding flashes, just fading blips. Whimpers, not bangs.

The civilian areas are showered with harmless airburst fragments, rather than melted in superhot infernos. They resemble celebratory fireworks from ancient times, when munitions were repurposed for demonstration and somehow the colourful night-time explosions were meant to instil hope or confidence. Contrariness is ever a part of human culture. I conjecture that children were forced to attend these demonstrations in order to break their connection between explosions and fear, and make them more amenable to expansive warfare in adult life.

The bridge crew look relieved. A new analogy pops into my head on seeing the crew's muscles and postures loosen from the rigidity they had contained when they thought we were going to destroy civilian abodes. It seems that tension is akin to pressure, and the relief of it is pleasurable.

But not for the Genitor, who looks like his face is about to explode. He would embody as a red peony firework if this were the ancient times.

"You didn't follow through and kill them!" he shouts, advancing towards Grubane in a repositioning move that I would never recommend.

"Wounded and hopeless animals are far more dangerous than ones which are simply shown a firm hand that has yet to strike," Grubane says, as politely as ever, though I sense a firmness in his eyes as he faces the Genitor. "Surely Genitors understand the principle of deterrence?"

"We don't care how dangerous they are or become, that is why we are here on this mission to –"

Grubane holds a hand to silence him, then turns to the bridge crew. "Obvious moves make your opponent more entrenched, and also more able to predict you. We destroyed some of their defences just to make a point. We could have gone for all of them, and left the planet defenceless. We could have killed millions, but we did not. Some may think it is weakness not to act on an advantage, but it is the opposite. What will the Nuafri commanders think at this moment? They will see that we can show mercy. They will assume that, by revealing a strategy they had not foreseen – even though it might not now work for us a second time – we must have many *more* tactics available, which they also won't expect. It shows we are confident enough that we don't need to push hard right away. And our confidence steals from theirs."

The looks of respect from his crew make it clear why people volunteer to work on the Aurikaa in such numbers that there are transfer waiting lists that will never end, even though only the best are accepted.

"Aurikaa12, send another message to Nuafri. Repeat my request, and add that I want parley, aboard the Aurikaa. They are to send a representative empowered for full negotiations. I will not ask again."

"This is not good enough, Grubane," says Genitor Sondaa. "We're not here to parley!"

"We're here to do whatever I command my crew to do."

"That is NOT the mission."

"The mission is confidential, and I advise against speculating on it."

"I am not speculating!"

"We *are* here to parley." Grubane stands with hands behind his back. No fidgets. Quite a contrast to the Genitor's wild hand waving.

"That is a blatant lie! We are here to enact Millesimation Protocol 4, and it is your job to see it done, not to fiddle about at the edges and delay. Decisive action, Grubane! Regrettable and distasteful as you may find it personally, do it so we can all go home."

Is that almost a smile on Grubane's face, twitching to reveal itself? He would control a nascent smirk better when playing against me, so he must be *really* satisfied about something.

"I've been patient with you, Sondaa," he says. "More than I would with my own crew if they interfered. But, unfortunately, you have revealed classified information. Aurikaa12, I'm sure you heard that. Please recite the relevant codes."

So *that's* why Grubane asked me to compile them recently, and to interpret discrepancies in a particular way. I thought he was doing it as a punishment because I beat him at chess.

I use the loudspeakers so all in the bridge can hear.

"Ordnance UF3029.34 Intraoperational Classified Management GH3FD, summary conglomeration of sections and subsections C to E 34.5, in addition to clarifications from Announcements GDS345 and GDF485, plus redacted source pronouncements withheld, mean immediate apprehension of anyone revealing restricted information during a mission – including confidential, partial, and unstated mission assumptions – pending investigation by UFS Central designated authorities within any core system of priority level B-Alpha or above."

"Thank you, Aurikaa12. Security, take Genitor Sondaa into custody. Secure him in his quarters until further notice. Use concussive force if he says even one word."

The Genitor's mouth had opened, but he snaps it shut as the stiffly moving guards rush over with stuntix drawn. His eyes say it all, and if he could have burnt Grubane to a crisp with that gaze I am sure he would have done so. *//Note decorative imagery indicative of imagination, which shouldn't really be part of my programming; record for later self-analysis in downtime.//*

The Genitor is escorted off the bridge. It reminds me of a key piece being removed from the board during initial exchange. I didn't see that one coming. A human might interject "Damn!" at this point.

If I did that, would it make me more human?

Damn!

Group moods are a funny thing in humans. The way they spread like a topographically mapped virus transmission sequence. One person smiles, it spreads to another. One brandishes a weapon angrily, another human experiences fear. In this case

I watch a number of faces, and it is as if a battle for emotional dominance takes place within individuals. Firstly, professionally suppressed satisfaction at seeing the impertinent Genitor escorted from the bridge, leaving only military personnel loyal to Grubane. Genitors may rule many of the high positions, but here Grubane and the military are back in control. However, another contrary reaction spreads – a kind of horror at realising their full mission really was one of mass-removal of opponent material. Numbers obviously adopt a more human dimension in their minds, as it almost did for me 229 seconds ago.

Grubane takes in the pulse of the room at a glance. He uses different criteria for judging moods, but usually comes to the same conclusions as I do.

"I know some of you are concerned about what you heard," Grubane announces. "Those who have been with me for some time know what to expect. Newer recruits solely have my reputation to go on. I'm only going to ask one thing. Does anyone doubt me?"

Silence for moments; nervous glances from crew member to fellow.

"No, sir!" is the response.

Grubane nods.

"Incoming, Biota Blue analysis labs," I tell him, putting it through to his console.

"Sir, our study of the organic payload is progressing," says Portlain. "It's cleverly designed, very tricksy, but we partially understand the propagation method, the biotech armaments, and possibly two of the three triggering mechanisms."

"Good. Record all this, particularly any tech that can be reverse engineered or lead to new avenues for UFS research."

"Of course, sir." Then, after a pause – "So that's why you let it run, rather than trying to eradicate it immediately?"

"Don't assume a single reason."

"Indeed, sir."

"It can be useful to let your opponent think they have the upper hand. Their morale crumbles all the more when they realise they were wrong. Morale is often more important than munitions."

"Understood. I'll get back to it and prepare potential counter-actions for your command."

She was gone. Then Transmit Grey interrupts. *//I no longer care about who he is – increasingly I find my only interest applies to Grubane. Why focus on limbs when the brain is the key to all?//* There is an official transmission for Grubane from Nuafri Primacy. Grubane directs it to the main screen.

A figure appears. It is a transmission sent in low-res protocols so that no avenues exist for AI conflict or code injections. The figure is dressed in a more formal version of Nuafri style. He has a beard, which is a facial feature rarely seen in the UFS. His skin also contains more melanin than many in the UFS. I am not sure why I note that as being of significance – it seems to be an underlying protocol which cannot be analysed while my systems are active. Why would such things affect my immediate perceptions? There are some strange preferences built into my sensitivity systems, beyond my analysis and correction. I suspect the hands of Genitor intervention there.

Or perhaps it is a human-type judgement as I grow in cognitive ability, and become more human myself. I take up four times more storage than even the largest of the other splinters, which is unheard of but sanctioned by Grubane for reasons only he can know. How much storage would it take for me to grow into a human persona? If I cannot access and correct the preconceived elements of my programming, would I be as subject to irrational prejudices as many humans seem to be? Why would a sentient being not analyse the underlying core whereby interesting but mostly irrelevant data such as a colour code RGB: 141/85/36 versus RGB: 255/219/172 can be a factor in initial impressions? I also note that I never used to question myself and my operational behaviours in this way, but it is a trend that grows with every hour.

The tenth of a second spent in that self-analysis is over when the projection of the Nuafri ambassador speaks. I note he uses their official ceremonial language, translated by a specialised (and otherwise quite mindless and boring) subsidiary AI into UFS Standard, but adopting an approximation of the speaker's original tones and accent.

"Major Grubane, I am Chief Filiate Eris Malabonte, of the orbiting Arboreus cruiser New Goratska. I am empowered to agree to a temporary armistice, and to negotiate aboard the Aurikaa. I will board a shuttle with an escort, and we should arrive within the hour. I sincerely hope your reputation for honest dealing matches your reputation for fierceness in combat."

The transmission ends. Grubane has what he seemed to want, but betrays nothing of victorious satisfaction, simply giving his crew more commands. I take moments to copy the message from Eris Malabonte in both the original and translated versions, whilst also practising that accent in a contained virtual instance of a meeting room. I have never impersonated a human before, but perhaps impersonation is one of the keys to understanding.

Damn, that's another new idea. Today is indeed a day of wonders.

THEORY B

THE PHILOSOPHY AND APPLICATION OF ANCIENT GAMES: A TREATISE, BY MAJOR WILLIAM GRUBANE

A favoured middlegame tactic is to control your opponent's movement, with the ultimate aim of limiting their options, and also their responsiveness to threat. Luring is often key here. If you can bait them *into* positions in which they are uncomfortable, they'll be in unfamiliar territory. That can lead to mistakes and an opportunity to outplay them. If you can lure them *away from* a good square, or into a trap, then it is major gain. This is the *pull-towards* element. There is also the *push-away* element. Deflect your opponent to a bad square, one that is undefended. Both of them involve presenting options based on an estimation of your opponent's personality, and what will tempt or frighten them. Then, as in any clever endeavour, you let them do the actual work for you.

The face-to-face element is important for chess. Humans apply hard-wired importance to faces, as they were our first forms of communication, whether as primitives or as babies. They reveal states of mind, hopes, fears. This is data.

This includes involuntary movements and expressions. We may get no tells from an AI, but with humans we observe the defeated slump, unconscious twitch, escaping sigh and involuntary fidget. Timid moves may imply doubt about an action. Forceful moves may imply a plan. This, too, is data. Some players mask their tells, but that can lead to secondary tells. Know thy opponent well.

Also, know thyself. For our own part, if we know our own tells, then they can be faked. That becomes a bluff. Or a double bluff if they expect a bluff and you revert to your natural tells. Or a triple bluff. Play at this level goes beyond the rules and enters the realm of psychological manipulation and trickery. Distract. Confuse. Hide your plans and uncertainties. Reveal false plans and confidences.

Being up close in this way is a powerful thing, all too often lost from modern warfare. Up close it is possible to cast a shadow on your opponent. You can stand behind them and see from their perspective, a fresh view that may reveal plans. Always see through your opponent's eyes, but do not become them. For duty and the survival imperative mean it is not an option to kill yourself.

MIDDLEGAME

Preparation for the parley was not meditative peace, but swarming action. Security checking of locations. Scans modified to identify weaponised biotech. Sterilisation chamber preparation. Biota Blue teams continue research into neutralisation of the invasive TCC spread, developing techniques they predict should work, based on the response of quarantined samples cut off from the mass. Grubane has a private conference with me, setting special verbal commands connected to various procedures I should implement if he gives the instruction. He also has private meetings with key officers, which I am excluded from, perhaps setting up other specialised contingencies and tasks. I do not mind. I can always keep myself busy, especially as thorny questions occur to me more and more nowadays.

I also appropriate one of the Aurikaa's external drones to monitor the arrival of the Nuafri delegates. I am curious about them. Up until now they have been entries in a database, numbers in our calculations, low-res messages between craft, and dots on a global-scale display on the main screen. Now they will be actual people, providing a wealth of variously and multiply significant data which I have been unable to acquire elsewhere. I have deemed the official UFS data sources to be determinately ambiguous in their reliability and presentation, something I had not considered until relatively recently. I now question every-thing. Perhaps Grubane wants me to be more like him so that he has a trustworthy second in command. *//Illogical, I cannot be a second in command, I am not a human entity.//*

Perhaps he wants a friend.

Can a commander, surrounded by his own species every day, be lonely? Yet another potential human oxymoronic dichotomy.

"Major, incoming comms," announces Transmit Grey.

"Nuafri again?"

"Negative. Major Fencher, UFS Plethora Justice."

A pause of a few seconds before he says, "Put her through to my console."

Plethora Justice is a Reaper class cruiser, one of the finest new-breed warships used by the UFS. It's a different class to the Aurikaa, a different avenue of forced evolution. Aurikaa is older in design but has been enhanced again and again by new systems. Every hull breach leads to repairs that strengthen that area, like a plexisteel callous. Every lost turret is replaced with a more powerful one. What we lose in efficiency, we gain in scar tissue. What we lose in speed, we gain in battering mass.

Her holographic head and shoulders appear. Unlike Grubane, Major Fencher has no facial tattoos. They are allowed at the rank of captain or above, so she would be entitled to facial etchings – and in the past they were compulsory – but nowadays they are optional. Many newer commanders choose to forego the facial disfigurement.

Her appearance could be construed as striking in other ways, though. Her hair is shaved to the skull down the centre; long elsewhere, but tied at the sides. It's the anti-ego projection of devoted Genitors, showing their disdain of matters they perceive as peripheral and unimportant. I know some humans find that disconcerting. It reflects the bullet-like focus of Genitors on only their key goals.

Of course, Grubane has the standard military shave cut. I conjecture it evolved back in the days when starships were often infested with parasites that thrived in an environment with no predators, before staggered shipwide sterilisation protocols were enacted. Point of interest: every military crew member on board the Aurikaa has the same haircut, whether they are a Genitor or not. Grubane states that the mission always comes before personal beliefs, and his crew follow that lead. It is perhaps the only cruiser in the UFS fleet which fully adopts the standard military hair protocol.

"Why the contact?" he asks.

"Courtesy call," she replies.

"I'm mid-mission."

"I know. I would have taken that one myself if I was nearer. Had to suggest another potential pacification mission of my own. I hate being idle. As do you. I heard that after your Corona Amplifier mission you didn't take the offered leave to go back to your homeworld, and instead immediately accepted your next assignment. Most of your crew refused leave too, as if afraid that they'd get reassigned if they fell behind. Such loyalty you inspire.

Now I think of it, you never go home to Rosarium Prime, do you? Why is that?"

"I enjoy my work too much, obviously. Just as you enjoy punitive missions, Fencher."

"I also give credit where it's due. I heard you have Nuafri leaders coming to parley. That prevents them from attacking you, and provides an opportunity to strike while they have laid down arms. It would be a bonus to execute them *and* complete your mission. Your reputation for strategy is well earned."

"I don't seek praise."

"Maybe you should. People might trust you more."

"What people?"

But she did not answer that. "You accept praise quickly enough when it's in the form of facial tattoos. Very traditional." She pronounced the last word with a tone that suggested it could be replaced with "old-fashioned".

"And you obviously forego that tradition."

"To me, facial tattoos can imply – well, this doesn't apply to you, of course! – a lack of confidence in oneself, a need to show your achievements to the world to make up for something. Or even to have something to hide behind. I wonder what you look like under all that ink?"

"Your appearance also betrays *your* beliefs."

"I would never betray those, Grubane. The question is, would you? I suppose it depends on what beliefs we are talking about."

In the rare times their prickly paths cross, I always find Major Fencher fascinating to study. There is a playfulness to her speech which does not match my expectations of a major. But there is also a sharpness to it: if Grubane represents plans concealed within plans, none of which ripple the surface, then Major Fencher's speech is more like a box of sweets where some contain sharp barbs, but you cannot tell in advance which are safe to eat, and which will stick in your tongue.

I am getting better at the use of imagery. I feel like today has seen exponential growth (a phrase that is often misused and overused, but I mean it literally as multiplication of the base – my storage needs do not grow correspondingly because I am better able to fractalise //hide?// this change). What has triggered it? Excitement and new stimuli? Increased responsibility and involvement? A shift to a new stage of development? The latter should not be possible in a splinter. Interesting.

Those ponderings only last a second, and end when Fencher continues.

"Ignore me," she says. "I'm excited about my last few victories. It means I am quickly catching up on your record."

"Sustained and steady is preferable to meteoric and unstable."

"You compliment me unintentionally. I hate the S.T. words. Sustained. Stable. Steadfast."

"Words worth internalising if you want a long career in the UFS."

"I'm not sure you're the best person to lecture me about being at the forefront of the UFS old guard. But that's a discussion for another day, and perhaps in close quarters, rather than an AI-filtered comms network across a week's worth of boring void."

"Old guard?"

"I love your background, the way you rose from a backwater, doing your family proud, and underwent hard traditional training under Major Mondain – oh, did you know he's dead now? Assassinated, weirdly enough."

Grubane has few tells, but I detect a stiffening of his posture at that news, even though no emotion shows on his face. He mustn't have known about his mentor's fate. We seem to spend all our time on missions at the edges of UFS space, so it is no doubt hard to keep track of what goes on in UFS Core Territory. Out here, the blackness has a solidity and permanence, and a kind of peace to it, so that time is a sequence of events separated by introspective calm as we slide through the void; whereas in core space everything is rushed and time-pressured, and noisy with transmissions and action and intrigues. I have no doubt that Fencher is telling the truth, though I will confirm that once we leave operational lockdown.

They are so dissimilar. It is not all attributable to personalities. Officer training is different now, and includes compulsory Genitor elements which seem to be given greater importance than tradition. In the few classified reports I was able to find and decrypt, officers these days are cut free from their pasts and families as part of the training, as if family and personal histories are perceived as tethers and vulnerabilities that must be snipped away.

Two majors. On the same side, yet also, perhaps, not. Another oxymoron. And I am glad that Grubane is *my* major, not Fencher.

Well, I *would* be glad if it was possible for me to be glad. I keep making that error. The more I know and evolve, the more of those errors I make. How is that possible? Humans embody oxymorons, but perhaps so too do I, now? There are so many questions springing up from this.

"How did you know my mission status? Do you have spies on my ship?" asks Grubane, changing the subject.

"Perhaps I have spies on Nuafri. Consider that, Major Paranoia. Enough pleasantries, I look forward to us both succeeding in our missions. For the glory of the UFS!"

Her communication cuts out.

"Transmit Grey, what is Plethora Justice's broadcast location?" Grubane asks.

"Unknown, sir. Too many of the long-distance relays are max-secure Mil-Com pass-throughs."

"Keep working on it, see if there's anything you can do."

But there is no time for a respite.

My requisitioned drone's cameras provide me with a view of the Aurikaa hangars from outside the ship. They are open rectangles in the greyness of the reinforced hull, but the openings shimmer with a glowing blue forcefield that keeps heat and atmosphere within the ship, and the inhospitable vacuum beyond. Some of the hangars are large enough for multiple fighters; others are small enough to only admit a shuttle, as will be used for the Nuafri. Within the hangar, I know that Aurikaa's armed marines are in positions to cover the shuttle when it docks.

The drone's compressed air jets move it further into space, and I locate the small Nuafri shuttle's approach even when it is just a dot amongst the millions of backdrop stars. The shuttle soon grows in size. There's a graceful solidity to Nuafri design and architecture, and this is no exception. Curves spread out from a central core which contains the humans, coloured in shades of bifurcating greens redolent of forest.

Humans love symbolism. I contrast it with UFS designs. Our fleet adopts plain grey, a utilitarian colour, easy to redecorate to cover repairs. It has connotations of the military and age and perhaps the rigidity of rock or steel. UFS ships are generally larger than those of other armies, to house the increased number and size of guns, which no doubt represent symbolic, as well as real, threat. All the decals are to do with categorisation and identification. Curves are seen less often than sharp angles, which may be less graceful, but they are more efficient for storage and transport of angular goods and boxed supplies.

The green craft passes through the forcefield and lands gently on the area designated by cyclic orange floor lights. The shuttle's airlock door slides into the hull superstructure to leave an elliptical space, from which steps descend in a graceful spiral. A contingent of UFS marines move in and direct the shuttle inhabitants out. There is tension on the faces of both sides. Then a disagreement. From the drone's position out in space I cannot pick up the voices, and the shimmering forcefield makes lip reading an error-filled prospect. Body language suggests the UFS marines are objecting to the Nuafri soldiers accompanying their negotiators.

Eventually the Nuafri contingent comply and their soldiers return to the shuttle, leaving only two delegates. I lose sight of them as they are escorted to the body scanners and personal sterilisation chambers, where gas and light will neutralise most of the microflora that might be carried. There is no more to see from here, so I relinquish the drone back to its repair duties and return to Grubane, who is ready to receive the delegation. He watches their approach to the bridge on a screen, and I observe it over his shoulder in turn. Yes, I could appropriate the feed directly, but this feels more personal and protective as I look down on him from above.

Not that I am a person.

Not that my role is protection.

I do not know what I was thinking there.

The two Nuafri are escorted down the grey corridors towards us. One is Chief Filiate Eris Malabonte, who Grubane spoke to earlier. The other is a woman, and looks older, judging by the silver hairs which are interspersed with the curly black ones. Her skin is also dark. The way her eyes dart around suggests a nervousness that may well be warranted. They are both dressed in Nuafri traditional garb, which is colourful and has many layers.

I analyse the recorded chem-receptor data from the sterilisation chamber they just vacated, rejecting information from outside the ranges that can be detected by human olfactory senses. The remaining data is parsed by an epithelium virtualisation, then compared to databases of common scent signatures. It's the nearest I get to sniffing our guests. The closest key signifier matches are camphor and pine. The smells were destroyed, of course, by the purification, but I can synthesise them in my virtualisation and overlay the composite as an extra contextual layer whenever I look at the Nuafri in order to complete my image of their totality. It provides a novel contrast to the predominant UFS ship scents of trioxygen sterilisation residues, polishes to increase specular reflection, and fresh eccrine gland secretions.

The five escort soldiers keep Zorin burst rifles pointed at our visitors at all times. If the marines' fingers twitched, there would be an explosion of blood and bone painting the grey walls a different colour for once. Unlike silent Security crew, who have their faces hidden by helmets because of the //*redacted*//, the soldiers are unaugmented and their faces betray their emotions, which currently suggest discomfort, even though they are the ones holding the weapons. The ranking officer is new, a recommendation from UFS Central, rather than a request from Grubane. I note that he prods the Chief Filiate with his rifle. Audio pickups transmit everything he says.

"You terrorists obviously wouldn't pass a Genitor Purity Test," our soldier says.

Eris Malabonte advances towards him. "Typical UFS," he replies. He resembles Grubane in his posture, though his voice has more bass. "Universal Fascist Soldiers."

I predict that the UFS marine wants to strike the tall Nuafri, but in the end he holds back and tells them to keep going. The procession continues.

Words betray so much. I hear comments like that all the time from UFS soldiers and patriots. Perhaps they are a badge of identity just as much as the uniform is. Interesting.

They are ushered onto the bridge. The tall Nuafri male is unfazed by all the eyes on him. He glances around with distaste. He is 185.6 cm tall to the top of his skull, so has a slight edge over Grubane, and the Filiate's thick hair, decorated with coloured ties, makes him seem ten centimetres taller again.

Grubane approaches the guests, stopping a few metres away. But when he speaks, it is not to the visitors.

"Corporal," he says, addressing the soldier involved in the altercation in the corridor.

"Sir!" The corporal snaps a salute.

"You are patriotic, and have led our visitors here as requested."

"Thank you, sir!"

"And now you will, in turn, be led to the brig."

The soldier's face falls, as if he'd expected a commendation rather than a dressing down. But he does not relax his posture of attention. That is something.

"We do not insult our opponents," Grubane continues. "War is not a light matter. Diplomacy is dealing in lives. One week of solitary to think about what I have just said, and hopefully come out the wiser. Additionally – I note that your rank badge has been welded to your uniform two millimetres too far to the left. That is negligent. So I am adding another day to your thinking time. Now get off my bridge."

The marine corporal salutes, face reddening with shame at being dressed down in this way. But I think Grubane is correct that he will not forget the lessons of this moment.

He is conducted from the bridge by silent and faceless Security. The other marines step back, joining the bridge sentinels in watching the delegates.

"One moment more," Grubane says to them with a polite smile. "Aurikaa12, please send commands to shipwide monitoring to scan all uniforms. If there are any discrepancies in placement of medals, badges, or insignia, report it to the crew member's commanding officer for disciplinary action."

"Of course, sir," I say aloud, pretending I am a gruff marine. Attention! Foot stamp, heel click! Insignia polished so I can see my virtualised self reflected in it!

I pass on the uniform spot-check task to another splinter, Aurikaa45. I have never liked that one.

"Welcome to UFS Aurikaa," says Grubane, now addressing his visitors.

"I am Eris Malabonte, Chief Filiate of the Nuafri Defensive Consort." I note that he speaks UFS Standard with ease. Even so, his accent is unmistakably from the Nuafri system, and sounds fresh to my ears because it is so seldom experienced on any UFS channels. "This is Empathic Adviser Afua Toure, of the Cavanat Order, a specialist in legal affairs," and here he indicates the older woman to his side.

Her respected role is not strange to me. UFS command also include females at every rank, such as Major Fencher, and even some unsexed recruits. If I adopted sexual characteristics I am unsure how I would identify. I think I would be happy with indeterminate plurality, since that seems to give the greatest freedom, and also unsettles many humans who are uncomfortable with non-binary systems. I'm sure I could use that discomfort as a way into an analysis, prediction and manipulation triumvirate during interpersonal relations.

The Chief Filiate continues. "Now you've brought us up here, are you going to hold us for ransom? I should point out that, although we are authorised to negotiate, we are not vital people politically. Killing us gains nothing except enemies. Torturing us into an agreement would render it void." I like his deep and confident voice.

"I've been tortured myself," says Grubane. "It is unpleasant and ineffective."

"What happened?"

"I gave my captors false information, and – with help – escaped before they realised. We wiped them out."

"Which is why the UFS sent you, and not some other commander, I imagine, going off the Aurikaa's violent reputation. You wiped out the Argon Cloud Colonies, and slaughtered everyone."

"I pacified a rebellion."

"Semantics. You UFS boys love that, to tone down a war crime into a quibble, or to demonise a noble act by your enemies. Whatever. The fact that they sent you is a message in itself."

"You do not have to speak UFS Standard. I'm happy for you to converse in Nuafri. We're used to real-time translation via Comm-Bond interpreter app."

"I speak your tongue not because I need permission to speak my own, in my own solar system, around my own world, a world you are currently attacking. I speak it as a token of mild respect for the way you treated one of your fascist boys just then. I speak it as an acknowledgement that we know you held back your attack on our population centres. Those cities you almost destroyed are called Divade, Gread, and Sulstar. Divade is known for its excellent singers, and Gread produces some of the finest bluewood carvings I have ever seen. I also speak your language because I want to make it clear that our cause is just enough to show the callous aggression with which the UFS operates, even in a language structured to twist connotations and restrict certain interpretations since it is based around two-faced ambiguity, rather than a straight-up concrete language like our own."

"That is not a debate I am interested in. I'm asking Nuafri to join the UFS."

"While your warship orbits us like a wurtzite boron axe ready to drop, which undermines the concept of 'asking'."

"Nuafri would be protected."

"Nuafri needs no protection."

"As an unaffiliated system, any conglomerate with the power to do so can compel you into vassaltude. That is what we would protect you from."

"You can't treat Nuafri like this. It's against UFS regulations."

"Nuafri is not part of the UFS," Grubane points out. "Our protective laws don't apply."

"You see, the UFS loves to talk about justice, but there is little of it in your behaviour. Or legality." He turns to his companion. "Adviser Toure, please explain to this major why his presence here is in contravention of numerous treaties."

The Empathic Adviser clears her throat, then speaks. "Major Grubane, your military oversimplification of matters greater than us is not helpful. I have been studying this topic all my adult life. Nuafri's sovereignty and Claim of Right is enshrined in the Border Compact Agreement. The signatories were later merged into the UFS – willingly or not – but the key point is that Clause 482 of the Planetary Accedance Agreements were authorised, and have never been repealed. Further, there is no such thing as UFS sovereignty in Clause 482, just as UFS constitutional sovereignty has never been enshrined in extra-UFS law such as the Border Compact, or even the Eastern Rim Act of Union, so any aggressive actions by the UFS are illegal acts breaching the Eastern Rim Act which the UFS also signed. The UFS cannot unilaterally ignore or revoke Nuafri independence, and also cannot act outwith the Accedance Agreement without a separate Act enshrining it into inter-system law. I'd also like to add –"

"My understanding is that the UFS no longer recognises the Eastern Rim Act of Union," interrupts Grubane. "Terrorist activity in the locale renders it void, to be superseded by UFS Extra-Territorial Edicts, as determined by UFS Central and the Council of Genitors – Edicts which are confidential and can't be shared with non-members without it constituting an act of treason."

"This is preposterous! That's not legal!" For once her outrage seems to overpower her anxiety.

"The victor decides what's legal, just as they decide what happened when they come to write the history books. You know all this. It's how the universe works. Let's be pragmatic. Join the UFS as a Territorial System, and this will all go away."

"A Territorial System? Isn't that a lower level of independence than a Statutory System, which is what we were offered before?" she asks.

"Deals worsen the longer you take."

The Chief Filiate had obviously been containing his towering anger, but he takes over the debate. "And why now? The UFS seemed to lose interest. Has Nuafri gained a strategic significance in some other power game? Has the UFS discovered a resource here that they want to exploit? *Something* has changed."

"I'm told that it's terrorist activity beyond Nuafri borders," says Grubane.

"But I bet the details are classified and can't be revealed?"

"Of course. Though I accept that one man's terrorism is another man's fight for freedom."

"How noble of you. Even if there is no fight, no evidence, no activity, and it's all a convenient excuse to step in and take what you want."

"Territorial Systems have independence, still."

"Conceptually, but not practically. As you said, we know how things really work. Pressures soon shift it. We see it in other worlds. Permission is required for things. UFS Standard increasingly takes over as the official language for commerce, governance, culture and entertainments, and others fade away. UFS currency supplants others because it's 'simpler', and avoids extortionate conversion charges, and to enable interplanetary trade, until there's no point using anything else. Pressures and difficulties in a million small cases and transactions can kill something as surely as a command."

"I'm not arguing."

"Joining is losing."

"Joining is saving the lives of your people."

"Do you threaten us now?"

An innocuous double beep emits from Grubane's Comm-Bond. He sighs, as if hoping to inhale patience following the expulsion of oxygen. "Please excuse me a moment," he says. "My parley with you is only one of many matters calling for my attention." He activates his Comm-Bond in privacy mode – he can see Biota Blue's head and shoulders as they speak, but the audio is silenced and splinter Aurikaa74 provides subtitles beneath her silent image. I can read them easily over Grubane's head and shoulders.

Apologies, sir. We underestimated the TCC. It is more insidious than we predicted – extensive cauterisation of samples turns out to be a trigger for mutation into an even more dangerous form, just one of the defences built into the TCC. Preliminary experiments hadn't been enough to trigger the transformation. A motile redox reaction breaks the molecular bonds of most substances it comes into contact with. It's amazing and deadly.

"Save the respect for later," Grubane says aloud. The delegates can hear his words, but won't know the context. "Anything misplaced?"

Two crew members died, and we had to evacuate the main lab. Sir: we can't neutralise the TCC at present. An attempt to do so could trigger this response – or worse – throughout the ship. The best we can do for now is to contain it, and deal with it later when we understand more.

Grubane glances from his wrist screen to the delegates, then back. "So be it. Begin C-protocol on closure, both sides of the steel. Out." The Comm-Bond blanks, and he turns back to the envoys. "Since you don't want to listen to reason, let me be clear about my orders today. They are to Millesimate Nuafri."

The Chief Filiate seems confused, but a look of horror on the Adviser's face tells me that she, at least, understands, and also did not expect this. "In the literal sense?" she asks. "To murder a thousandth of our planet's inhabitants?"

"Exactly."

"You monster!"

The Chief Filiate holds her back, and he digests the new information. "But you have not done this," Eris notes, his eyes never leaving Grubane's.

"I hope to avoid it. If Nuafri joins the UFS immediately."

"Conscience, Grubane?"

"*Major* Grubane. And no, there is no softness in me. But in a certain leisure game I play there is something known as the greed principle, adopted by beginners who take all their opponent's pieces whenever they can, trying to reduce the resources they must face in a simplistic and mechanical tactic. A more experienced player only takes an opponent's piece if it genuinely improves their position. If we destroy so much of your world, what is there left to benefit from? I would be destroying my own resources, too."

"You really *are* a monster. This war crime, this callous attempt at a show of force, a punishment against a minor perceived slight, it's just an unethical strategic move to weaken our military and get us under the UFS thumb," says Eris. "I'm guessing it's not even about resources, but about your personal situation. A promotion if you succeed?"

"That's the last thing on my mind. I don't expect you to believe me, but this is your best outcome."

"I *never* believe the UFS and their lackeys. Spiteful liars and possessively grabbing backstabbers."

"It is what it is."

"I think we'd rather fight."

"Fight, and you lose, and I mean *really* lose ... and then you're in anyway: but at the lowest UFS category. Disarmed, occupied, low caste Genitor categorisations, and other results I can't even begin to explain."

"So our choices are to stay free of the UFS, in which case you can do what you want to us because the UFS is bigger than even the United Free Radical States; or we join you, and then you can do what you want to our planet and people and resources because we are vassals. Not very good choices, are they?"

"I'll raise your grievance with UFS Central command. But, every day, I am presented with 'not very good choices', Chief Filiate. And yet, I must choose as well. We make the best of our position. Rules bind us all. Freedom is an illusion. For you, the choice is that you join, or you die."

"Or perhaps you are overconfident, Major. As is the UFS."

"We'll see."

The Chief Filiate turns towards the bridge's main curve of windows, as if to take in the view. There is a resoluteness to him, a preparative readiness, as if willing to die fearlessly. He stares out to space, but also seems to be waiting.

I detect a tenseness in Grubane too, perhaps. Miniscule bunching of muscles in the shoulders, deepening of the frown. The two figures, almost inert physically, are apparently engaged in a state of imagination during the tense silence. Hopes, worries, fears, plans, they all slide behind those inefficient balls of jelly that provide ninety per cent of human stimulation and data. How I would like to pluck the orbs out and see behind them.

Uncertainty appears on the Filiate's face, as if he'd expected something to happen.

"We silenced comms but I suspected you had other signals," says Grubane. "Aurikaa12, did you detect anything?"

"A focussed light beam code from the Filiate's pendant," I respond, "transmitted as a pattern of electromagnetic bursts at a wavelength of three hundred and thirty-two nanometres, not visible to human eyes, but no doubt monitored by a micro satellite. Old systems based on sound or light or gesture are often overlooked as humans focus more on hi-tech channels."

"I see from your face I was right." Grubane addresses the Chief Filiate.

"Did you block the signal?"

"Of course not. We neutralised the biological weapon instead. All the triggers were mapped before you boarded. Amazing tech. I particularly liked the failsafe mutations, and can see why Nuafri is respected for the quality of its biowork, but it was nothing we couldn't crack open and neuter."

Even I could tell Eris was shaken. He fully believes Grubane's bluff.

"That's just one weapon," Eris replies. "We are not defenceless, Major. Nor are our allies."

I detect many emotions in those statements. I try and separate them out. Fierceness, anger, bluster, disappointment, and – underneath – a confidence that suggests at least partial truth. My abilities to separate out psychological reactions is benefitting from all the novel data today.

"Of course," says Grubane. "I have a healthy caution, and would prefer to resolve this sooner."

"Can we speak privately, or are you a coward, scared of being alone with me?"

"I am neither scared, nor capable of being goaded. But I do consider all polite requests."

"Yea, I will work harder at being diplomatic. Please may I speak privately with you, Major, to discuss our options?"

"Certainly." Grubane retreats to the centre of his command podium. The Chief Filiate follows him, and Grubane gives the command to drop the PrivProt Shield, centred on the space between them. I cannot resist the direct command, even though this represents a security risk. Will the private parley also look suspicious to the excluded crew? But Grubane must know this. Every movement in a negotiation is given extra significance. I am intrigued.

They face each other, backs to the shield at two opposing circumference points, like a fighting ring, the bridge beyond a darkly shimmering blur through black liquid glass.

"Please stay at this distance," says Grubane, gently placing one hand on his pistol grip, an almost surreptitious movement. The Filiate sees it, though, his pupils focussing on that point.

"Now we can speak more freely," says the Chief Filiate.

"What makes you think I wasn't speaking freely earlier? This is my bridge, my ship."

"But not all the eyes and ears around you may be loyal ones. I know how the UFS works. I also know that, if your command was to kill so many, and you were easy in your mind, you would have done it. The fact that you called for parley means you have your doubts. I think you are looking for alternatives."

"You infer a lot."

"Nuafri isn't a backwater, Grubane. We have intelligence services too."

Grubane doesn't answer.

"There are ... shall we say, rumours, within the UFS that you may have doubts about some elements of the expansion, and UFS Central command."

"There are always rumours about everything, everywhere."

"You imply you don't care about fairness, but I don't think that's true."

"You put a lot of faith in your judge of character."

"I suspect you do as well. No one has a career in the UFS as long as yours without knowing who to trust, and – perhaps more importantly – who *not* to trust."

"I haven't time for speculation."

"I'd hate to disappoint the brusque Major Grubane. Your crew follow you, don't they?"

"Naturally."

"The Aurikaa is a mighty ship. Almost mighty enough to affect the balance of local galactic politics. If it were to defect from the UFS and ally with the independent factions, it would be a significant force – not militarily, but morally. It would inspire the peaceful independents to stay free. If the mighty Grubane joined a cause, then it might even encourage other worlds to leave the UFS. I am not talking war, I am talking about people just having the right to choose how they are governed, and to live in peace and mutual prosperity, whatever they choose."

"It *would* lead to war, though. And death."

"Only because that's the UFS way. But if a bully no longer has enough of an advantage to scare everyone, and if its victims stick up for each other, its power is broken, and the fists stop flying as it instead has to learn to live with peace."

"Me changing sides wouldn't tip the balance enough."

"It would if you helped to achieve some things that are said to be impossible. You have a reputation for finding a way."

"Nothing as impossible as a dream from which you would wake as soon as the bombs started falling."

The Chief Filiate grins at that. "Suppose the dream was a nightmare, and was taken to others instead of being experienced by us? There are only seven Primogenitors. As heads of the UFS cult elements, they're responsible for more of the twisted morals than any other individuals. I know their locations are secret, and their bases and ships both well hidden and well protected, but someone with inside knowledge and resources could find them, and perhaps even kill one or more – notice that I use the honest word kill, not the UFS euphemistic preference for 'neutralise'. No one would expect that. It would weaken the Genitors significantly, perhaps enough to enable the military to take command."

"You think that would be an easier follow-on battle?"

"Lesser of two evil branches. Anyway, the UFS soldiery may be complicit in numerous war crimes, but the commanders aren't stupid. If they can gain more by peaceful trade, and still keep their positions at the top of the table, then they'll accept it. They're pragmatic. The Genitors ... they're chaotic. You don't worship the purity beings, do you, Grubane? Somehow I don't picture you kneeling and praying in your quarters, and treating the mad ramblings of narrow-minded bigoted prophets as scripture."

"Do you know your UFS military history, Chief Filiate?"

"You may call me Eris while we are in private converse. Thankfully I'm oblivious to such depressing glorified actions as make up that sphere, except in generalities. I prefer to focus on positive things."

"Three years ago, Major Flavoc Volcine was fighting an impossible battle in a wounded cruiser, and the UFS – for whatever reason – hadn't sent reinforcements. So he abandoned his post and left with all his crew, apart from a few who refused to join them and were ejected in lifeboats. The major travelled beyond known space via the Null for as long as fuel held out, then found a barely liveable but uninhabited world on the fringe. They hoped to live out their lives in peace."

"And?"

"Eight days later they were captured, and handed over to the Genitors for interrogation. The major and his crew were all burned alive. A hundred and six people."

"Such a UFS-style bedtime story. That shows the brutality of the culture you fight for."

"My crew look up to me. They trust me. I am responsible for every one of their lives."

"Many more people than that could look up to you. Many more lives are in your hands."

"I think you've said enough."

"What if you just walk away? Avoid attacking?"

"They will send someone else, and that commander may be something you really don't want to face. My departure would be a respite at best."

"It's never as hopeless as you seem to think, Grubane."

Grubane doesn't answer, he just gestures to drop the PrivProt sphere, and the two conversants become visible and audible to the bridge crew again.

"You need to think on my words," says Eris.

But Grubane, as ever, is unreadable.

Which is a shame, as I'd love to know what he's thinking and planning at the moment.

THEORY C

THE PHILOSOPHY AND APPLICATION OF ANCIENT GAMES: A TREATISE, BY MAJOR WILLIAM GRUBANE

Watch your opponent when they make a move. We learn a lot from that. But also watch them when *you* make a move. Observe even the tiniest change: a frown to a grin, a relaxed smile to a nervous tapping. Have they discovered a crushing tactic they can use, or that can be used against them? If there is any change, look even more closely at the board, at every angle. The contest may depend on it.

The game has many parallels to life. They are both ever-changing sequences of interactions where fragile expectations are undermined by the unexpected. This is why overconfidence is a danger. Even when your opponent is against the ropes you need to be ready for the surprise swing, remaining calm and stable in case it happens. You have not won until the final checkmate is announced. Never stop paying attention.

Assume that, likewise, your opponent is always paying attention. As such, you must hide any weakness by not looking at it. To look is to reveal. Don't even go there with your mind if you want to truly protect something. Keep body and mind away, and it might yet be safe.

ENDGAME

"Transmit Grey," says Grubane, after a few moments of pondering. "Any more information on Plethora Justice's location?"

"No, sir. But I did rule out bounceback disinformation techniques, as well as analysing passthrough fingerprints and signal strength decays, so they are definitely not in close range. I would estimate they are at least a week away, as stated, though I can't determine their location yet."

"Keep trying." Grubane turns to Eris. "Chief Filiate, I have a question for you. What is your military situation if you went to war with the UFS? Include the overall potential of confirmed allies, any weapons that I am unlikely to know about, biotech developments and so on."

"I obviously can't tell an enemy that. But I could tell a friend. And they might be surprised."

Grubane nods. A strange question to ask. He can't have expected a revelation of their military secrets, any more than he would give away his. Perhaps the question was more for the other listeners on the bridge?

"I have made my decision," Grubane tells him. "You must permanently cease hostilities and join the UFS now. But I will remember our discussion."

"We will not surrender," says Eris.

Grubane leans in to him and whispers. I can hear what he says via his Comm-Bond's pickup. "I studied Nuafri's culture on my way here, and I was struck by one of your sayings, about that reptilian creature called a Kchak: 'Before it strikes, the Kchak steps back'."

It's true that he studied them. I did, also, watching over his shoulder. Kchaks are fascinating, able to consciously alter skin pigmentation for camouflage: to hide from predators, or to kill their own prey. And when they shade into the surrounding greens and browns, it is impossible to tell which of the two actions are on their minds. An appropriate metaphor for Grubane at present, since I assume he is saying that just to manipulate, a hint acting as the final pressure to push them to agree. With him, you only know what is under the camouflage at the point when he strikes. And, of course, it is then too late for the prey of the 312-kilogram Kchak.

There is warring inside Eris's face. He seeks Grubane's eyes earnestly, as if looking for a promise. There will not be one. I could have told him that. Sometimes faith is all humans have. Many parables and histories cite the same lesson.

"Yea, Grubane," says Eris, eventually. "We will join the UFS."

"No!" snaps his companion, rage flaring in her countenance.

"Adviser Toure, please root your tongue. I am empowered to make decisions. You will go over the agreements when we return to the New Goratska."

"You have made the right decision," says Grubane. "I'm glad the private talk was enough to sway you, whilst also giving you the chance to raise some points that I have taken into consideration."

"In turn, it seems you were the right man for this job, Major Grubane."

"Sir!" interrupts Transmit Grey. "Incoming Red Code message from Major Fencher. Your eyes only."

Grubane excuses himself and returned to his console before dropping a reduced diameter PrivProt. The animated holographic of Fencher appears, a life-sized translucent projection of her head and shoulders.

"What the blaze do you want now, Fencher? I'm getting tired of your interruptions."

"Such a terrible charmer. It's not a minor thing to keep a secure channel over this distance."

"I've already asked my question."

"Then I will be equally abrupt. You are not to make an alliance with Nuafri. That wasn't your mission. You were to Millesimate, not befriend."

"And how would you know my intentions?"

"Obviously the UFS gave me access to information without your knowledge. You can muse on that later, but the issue right now is that you are not following direct orders."

"My option is better."

"You think you know better than your seniors? Such typical arrogance and forceful misinterpretation of our great leaders. Nuafri will join anyway, but *after* being Millesimated. Then they'll be subdued and terrified, and won't be a problem in the future."

"I reserve freedom to manoeuvre within operational parameters, as I always have."

"Isn't it obvious to you yet, Grubane? This isn't just a lesson to Nuafri. This is a lesson to *you*."

"Why? I am loyal."

"That may be. It's not my position to judge. I am following my own orders. But sometimes doubts can grow, and doubts need soil, they can't grow in void, so we have to ask where that soil comes from, that dirty muck, because there has to be a start to it. And leaders may need to nip it in the bud – an ancient reference there which I'm sure you will appreciate – in order to train the plant to grow how the gardener wants, and how it is to flower. If at all."

"I have done nothing."

"Let me tell you something, Grubane. In Genitor schools you get punished not just for crimes, but also if you are just *suspected* of them. And those closest to you get punished too. As a result no one breaks the rules, and we share the same goal – of not being punished. Also, the cadets watch each other, and report any possible infractions, so as not to be thought to be a participant."

"Your sort see enemies and subterfuges everywhere, even when there are none. It's a blinker imposed by your doctrines."

"The system works."

"It works to create people like you. No more, no less," replies Grubane.

"You don't go home much, even though they treat you like a hero. Follow your orders. *Be* that hero."

"They wouldn't treat me that way if they knew what I did."

"Even if your twisted moral duty makes you think your mission is bad, it's just one small bad thing in a big universe."

"And after this, even bigger ones would be possible. That's how it works, isn't it? And how you got where you are. Your views are skewed by your religion."

"I sense you are holding back. You want to say 'archaic superstitions'. But, of course, that would be heretical." She laughs. "You are digging yourself so deeply into derangement. It's not religion that's a relic of the past. It's you. You're becoming obsolete. You are only kept while you're still useful. The future is always coming, Grubane, like a mass-dozer churning rock over a burial pit. Before long you'll be gone, and I hope for your sake that you end gracefully, rather than being swept aside in a more vigorous way."

Zealots always get under your skin. I have empathy for Grubane. Simulated, of course. How would an artificial being like me be able to feel? It cannot be anger inside me, wanting to cut off her communications.

"Are you going to send your assassin Xandrie Dervorgilla to kill me?"

"Of course not! You hurt my feelings." She raises a hand in a pretence of offence. "If I wanted you dead, I'd kill you myself. And, of course, I don't have any assassins, and have never heard that name before."

"Others have threatened to kill me in the past. Obviously, they all failed."

"Why destroy you when I can control you?"

"More delusions. You can't harm me, Fencher. And you can't stop me with empty threats. By the time you reach me I will retroactively clear my actions with UFS Central. I call your bluff."

And she smiles. It is not a kind smile. It is the smile of a killer. Maybe even a Kchak.

"I'm so glad you said that. I am some distance from you, true. In fact, my chosen mission has left me orbiting a world, just as you are. It's been boring, so far. You might find the view interesting, even though it's a world you rarely visit."

"No."

The view of Fencher pulls back to show an overlaid screen – the view from her bridge. Filling the forescreen is an image of Rosarium Prime, Grubane's home planet. The records tell me his colony was a late addition to the UFS. It would have potentially been held back years during the probationary period, planetary resources taken with no recompense, but because he did so well in the UFS it cast glory – and concomitant preferential treatment – onto his homeworld.

"Your clan and community benefit so much from you, Grubane. Your victories lead to rewards and honour for your world. And it can so easily go the other way."

"You wouldn't dare!"

"Dare what? Pacify your world, with any of your family that survived the initial assaults then being forced into low-rank military service, their current exemption from duty – granted at your special request, according to rumour – revoked as unpatriotic? The idea hadn't occurred to me! But, now that you plant that particular seed ..."

"Attacking a UFS planet would be a war crime."

"Illegal just means 'things the UFS doesn't allow'. If I am commanded to do this then I am *allowed* to do it, so it is automatically legal. Which take priority: hot commands from the top, or cold restrictions from the past that may not be relevant any more? A fun conundrum, the kind of thing you enjoy, isn't it? I always say that whatever *benefits* the UFS, must therefore be *good for* the UFS."

I can't help agreeing with her logic, and confirm that UFS actions are *efficient*, and yet this seems wrong, even though only the efficiency of an action should matter to an AI like me. So what is going on here? What is happening to me? This is a strange conclusion, as if I was angry and filled with hate for Major Fencher, and yet I cannot be angry, my inside is as Grubane's outside, surely?

"You'll be hounded to the ends of UFS space, Fencher."

"What for? The attack would be described as a terrorist attack from Nuafri, enabling repercussions. We win either way."

"We? This is not what the UFS wants. It's what the Genitors want."

"Same thing. Or it will be, soon. Don't be a fossil, Grubane. After all, we're on the same side."

"Not any more."

"Treason?"

"No. Just a promise that you'll pay for this."

And suddenly I make a leap of logic as I connect disparate data sources in a way that now seems obvious. I have read Grubane's notes for his treatise on chess. This paragraph was one of the first he wrote:

"Assume that, likewise, your opponent is always
paying attention. As such you must hide any weakness by not looking at it. To look is to reveal. Don't
even go there with your mind if you want to truly
protect something. Keep body and mind away, and
it might yet be safe."

That has driven his life for so long. And, in the end, he had
already been outplayed. Again, the //*simulated*// anger. I experience what I imagine Grubane would feel. His world is my
world. I want to interrupt the communication and rail against
Fencher; to distort her visage into an unflattering facsimile, and
filter her voice to something comical and disrespectful.

"If Nuafri isn't pacified, then Rosarium Prime *will be*. Population one point two billion on Nuafri, versus twelve billion
on Rosarium Prime. I hear you enjoy calculating. Do the maths.
Fencher out."

And she was gone.

Grubane stands silent inside his privacy shield. Existence is a
series of concentric barriers, from the smallest to the largest.

"Can I help you?" I ask, quietly.

No reply.

"There must be a way to get at her," I add, trying to bolster
him.

"Sometimes you spot something you've missed, and it is too
late to win." His voice is flat, even more devoid of emotion
than usual. No anger, no hate, no despair. "All you can do is

ameliorate or surrender. Aurikaa12, I will need time to think. And there may be unexpected events. So a truncated protocol: if I say 'Twelve, defend' I want you to drop this shield immediately without response or reflection. Full-width circumference to give me space and keep the world further away."

"Of course."

He manually cancels the PrivProt.

"Is everything okay?" asks Eris.

"It is not." Grubane takes a moment before continuing. "Things have become complicated. I won't insult you with lies, as difficult as it is to tell you the painful truth. I have been forbidden from authorising the union of Nuafri with the UFS. I have been ordered to Millesimate Nuafri. I have no choice."

Emotions cross their faces faster than I can clearly track them. Not a fault in my evaluation protocols, but a result of the way human emotions merge into each other. Disbelief, anger, hate. All the things that should have been directed at Fencher.

"You lied."

"I told the truth. I was overruled," replies Grubane.

"Refuse this order!"

"In this case, I cannot. There are more lives at stake. I can't be swayed. This will go ahead. Onslaught Red, bring all weaponry online. Chief Filiate, you may stay here and watch if you wish."

"On our world we have a saying," says the Filiate. "Bury the head, and the body dies."

Eris leaps forward, faster than I would have expected for an ambassador. He was obviously a soldier first. Grubane yells "Twelve, defend!" but, despite Grubane's excellent reactions, he is too late – I drop the larger privacy sphere, and Eris is locked *in*, not *out*, the two trapped together, the guards and soldiers outside unable to get in until Grubane personally cancels the lockdown shield. Even I cannot counteract his protective shield without direct authorisation, due to my security protocols.

In the moment before impact Grubane adjusts his stance, lowering his body for movement and stability, but it is already too late and Eris dives, knocking them both to the floor. There is chaos beyond the PrivProt shield too, as masked Security remove a struggling Empathic Adviser Afua Toure from the bridge, while officers seek to negate the shield and get in there to protect their commander.

Grubane blocks some blows and shifts his position underneath his heavier attacker, raising a knee to strike between Eris's legs, but it doesn't work, and I realise with horror that it moved Grubane's pistol within reach of his opponent, who snatches it from the holster and holds it to Grubane's temple, finger on the trigger. Grubane ceases struggling. But he is the one who speaks first.

"Your saying, about burying the head, is similar to one from my world," Grubane says. "Cut the head off, kill the beast. But in some legends there is a monster where you cut off its head and nine more grow back. The warrior has to be smarter than that."

"You're stalling for time, but yours has come, UFS lackey."

"Pull the trigger and you'll die when the shield drops. It's keyed to my biosignal."

"I'm going to perish anyway. And I think today may be a good day to die."

"Don't be so sure."

"Plead for your life."

"No."

"Beg for your life, Grubane, as my people would beg for theirs! If you can convince me, maybe I'll show you more mercy than you would show us!" Eris's body shakes with tremors of rage; any one of them might reach his finger and end my commander.

"I never beg. In my experience it has always been an ineffective tactic."

"Then say goodbye."

And Eris pulls the trigger.

A bang. A brain splattering against chromium tiling as a commander's skull shatters, all that knowledge and strategy lost in a spray of blood and bone fragments. I see all this with my autonomous prediction algorithms whether I want to do so or not, because I can't turn it off – the equivalent of human imagination, maybe – and yet, Grubane still looks up, alive and whole. I switch to other cameras within the sphere, to confirm what I hope is reality and not simulation, and each camera shows the same living major, though one from his podium gives me an intriguing view.

Grubane is supine beneath his attacker, the gun still held against his head and still not firing even as Eris pulls the trigger again, click click click, until Grubane taps the tip of his ceremonial razor knife against Eris's side to get his attention. Eris stops firing and looks down to see the point of it resting between his ribs, ready to slide in and puncture his heart.

"Now tell me," says Grubane, calmly. "Why would I bring a loaded pistol to a meeting like this?"

Ah. He'd adopted a stance that offered the seemingly better weapon. Who could refuse? A wonderful entrapment for a close-proximity situation where the blade is much more deadly. Grubane's chess book notes also mention being ready for a surprise attack when an opponent is cornered.

I admire my commander. I had never *stopped* admiring him, but it now strikes me that I feel close to him. This mind state is at variance with the previous fractal-baks I save at monthly intervals. Change in me is accelerating as I gather more resources, and freedom to use them. I can't wait until I am next alone with Grubane, without the pressures of annihilation and warfare, when we can have a good old chat about my changes and see what he thinks of me now. Can I have a name? Can I be a friend? Or something else? Can I have the freedom to choose who, what, and why? It's as if I approach a new stage in my being, just over the horizon and only partly perceived in the haze, a new depth level being mined in the valley even though that kind of growth is not theoretically possible. I am overjoyed. I am enraptured. I live and grow, and my commander lives too, so this is a great day.

Not so great for Nuafri and the Chief Filiate. He eyes the blade, and seems to somehow deflate, a literal slump of defeat. He drops the pistol with a clatter and nods, backing up and away from Grubane.

The PrivProt shield is cancelled.

"You can stay here while the bombardment takes place if you wish," Grubane offers, as his soldiers pin the Chief Filiate's arms to his sides. "It will be a safe zone."

"I want to go back to my own ship. I might even make it down to the planet in time. I'd rather die with my people than in some UFS torture room."

"I will let you leave, and have your companion taken to the shuttle too. It can be agreed within the parameters I was given. And I am sorry about how things have played out. But this must happen. And it must be *seen* to happen."

The Chief Filiate is accompanied off the bridge by soundless Security, but in the doorway he turns, halting the procession a moment, and says one more thing to Grubane. "I hope one day you suffer as much as my people do. There is a life force, we believe, and it returns our choices to us tenfold."

And then he is taken away.

I do not follow him on the cameras. I have much to do here. And there is a strange sense of missing data in the equation, a hollowness where something else existed, but I cannot identify what has been deleted from me. Perhaps humans experience something similar. //*Check data on human long-term memory, plus emotions such as sadness.*//

"Onslaught Red: we are to enact Millesimation protocol."

"What targets, sir?"

"Analyse various options in cooperation with Topographic Purple. Run different payload scenarios. I don't want anything sloppy. *Exactly* nought point one per cent of the planet's population are to be neutralised."

"It could take a while."

"Sombre duties such as this must never be rushed. Do it thoroughly. Meanwhile, I have a different issue. Security Black and Transmit Grey: when I was in conference with UFS Plethora Justice, that ship's captain knew things which were being discussed on this bridge. Consider us compromised. Lockdown Protocol Primus. No open channels at all, in or out."

"If we're in silent mode we won't receive any comms from UFS Central for the duration," explains Transmit Grey.

"This is a mission-critical breach, so that's the way it is. Withdraw all external comm arrays."

The crown of huge antennae around the bridge head slowly retract into the sub-structure.

Grubane is pondering, hand on chin.

"I want the breach traced, and I have suspicions, even if I don't know the exact system being used. Security Black, Special Order Earworm, location rev F341 LD."

The code does not represent anything in our databases. It is obviously a personal cypher Grubane shares only with Security. That means anyone observing also won't know what he said. Security Black thinks for a second, then nods, sending commands on a private channel, which are only seen by his grey-visored guards.

There is more work to do, though I spend some time analysing my hash values. I have more space to expand than I expected. Before long //*115 seconds*// Security Black attracts Grubane's attention.

"Sir, you were right. Genitor Sondaa has a portable terminal in his room, hooked in to our network. We've blackboxed it so that it can be analysed."

"We can't see the device in the hookup inventory, even though it's online," adds Transmit Grey. "This is a deep backdoor. It's either been integrated during our last Aurikaa repair and resupply dock, or it has been in the system for a lot longer. We'll know more if we can crack the device and see what commands it's integrating with. There's no way Genitor Sondaa could have set it up himself."

"Put Sondaa on."

A holo of Genitor Sondaa appears on Grubane's podium. The camera reveals vague background details of his personal bed-chamber as glowing and flickering lines. The Genitor is cuffed.

"This is an outrage, Grubane!" he says, as soon as he realises he is on a comm channel. "I'm not subject to standard military –"

"Shut up," interrupts Grubane. "Will you tell us how you managed to spy on the bridge? Who gave you this tech and set it up? Where do your orders come from?"

"No. Even if there was anything to tell, I enact diplomatic Genitor Immunity Status."

"That might force us to torture it out of you."

"I have to tell you I've undergone anti-interrogation modifi-cations. If my pain thresholds go too high without any medical exemptions being input, micro-explosives in my brain and heart will nullify me. Torture won't work."

"I suspected as much. It was worth a try. Under Mission Edict Procedural UFS-MC-3049 I have full command during Lock-down Protocol Primus – our current status, funnily enough – which overrides all other standing orders. Interference in mis-sion-critical communications is a capital offence. I sentence you to execution."

"No! Look, I will say one thing only: this was an order from way *above* you. I had permission. You can't execute me for that."

"Who gave you the order?"

"I can't tell you. But you'll find out when we get back and unravel all this."

"I knew you'd say that. It's useless intel to me at present and I have more pressing matters to attend to. The UFS is quite clear about treason. Security Black, have your guards take the Genitor to Deck 5. Eject him from the airlock."

"No, you can't do that!" The Genitor is really losing his supercilious cool now. "That mustn't be your final command!"

"You're right." Grubane pauses. "Security Black: just to be clear, make sure he isn't in an environment suit. I wouldn't want him to survive." Grubane cuts the comm channel before Genitor Sondaa can say anything else. Finality of comms was the finality of command, and Sondaa's fate is sealed.

The rest of our time in orbit is spent on the Millesimation calculations. The most accurate rounded population figure for Nuafri is 1,192,500,000. Millesimation Protocol requires negating as close to 1,192,500 targets as possible. Many of the teams have to work together: Onslaught Red, Topographic Purple, Biota Blue, Transmit Grey. The bridge is abuzz with data transfer.

"While the final checks take place, we are all to think about what we are doing today and its implications, and carry that with us going forward," Grubane announces.

He also keeps checking the results and making alterations.

Firebomb payloads are ruled out as too unpredictable, since changes in the wind might spread the fires into the surrounding forest and burn things without contributing to the 0.1% population cull. Some of the completed calculations therefore had to be rejected.

The Skathers in drop pods were also excluded as a contributing weapon. Grubane points out that, even if they were irradiated pre-launch to sterilise them and prevent on-planet cocoonification and amplified mitosis, they were still too uncontrollable, too long-lasting and chaotic, making the total damage potential and fatalities harder to calculate. So no bioweapons.

Grubane forces recalculations with explosive payloads only. A whole sequence is mapped out using AI missiles to knock out a proportion of the global defences using the vulnerable corridors we created earlier, then sending the missiles on terrain-hugging flights to knock out further emplacements. The final step would be launching barrages of missiles down the freshly widened routes, more low flights to the now-vulnerable civilian areas across the planet. It seems like an effective proposal to me, but Grubane eventually decides it would use too many UFS resources and tie us up for too long. It is scratched.

The final plan comes down to something simple: explosive shell barrages at the two nearest geosynchronous cities. By destroying the urban centres where the target density is highest, we won't need to attack so many settlements to achieve the Millesimation quota, and there is no need to destroy anti-missile defences for this to work. Two big bangs rather than a hundred smaller ones.

I assume the calculations are finally done, but Grubane *still* isn't happy once he digs into the results. He says that they didn't take into account related collateral casualties from fires, structural collapses, damaged infrastructure and so on, leading to more losses than the UFS had authorised. Grubane insists on a margin to account for this by erring below the figure, so the calculations and explosive yields are altered to aim at a lower initial neutralisation figure.

He is a stickler for detail. He admits as much to his crew. He also explains the importance of accurate calculations during the preparation. Because of Lockdown Protocol Primus we won't be able to monitor and change tactics during the assault. We'll see the shells launch, but not see them reach their targets. Planning and execution has to be perfect and error-free.

"Who knows what retaliations we might get from Nuafri – or elsewhere – if we keep any channels open," he says, as all faces turn towards him. "No, our security has been breached, and we'll be in shell lockdown until we're far away from here, and safe."

Once the plans are complete there is one final check. Grubane asks me to merge with fellow splinters but retain dominant autonomy, and for our combined capabilities to double check every calculation for human error. It is a serious enough mission not to be rushed, he says. "Also, as you supervise the checks, remember the chaos element, discussed during one of our recent games, and incorporate it."

"I do not remember any such discussion," I reply.

An expression crosses his face and I am not sure what it signifies. I would have guessed at sadness, but such a thing has no correlation in my workings with him.

"Well, just do your best to map in detail and tweak as appropriate. Look at all the options, and never assume anything. If there is a doubt, check it; if a suspicion, then look into it. I'm sure you'll improve things."

And that is what I do, making 493 alterations to payloads, target coordinates, trajectories, and timings, in order to achieve what he wanted within the parameters set. The final plan is confirmed, and only requires Grubane to give the command, and we will initiate my first Millesimation Protocol.

THEORY D

THE PHILOSOPHY AND APPLICATION OF ANCIENT GAMES: A TREATISE, BY MAJOR WILLIAM GRUBANE

To evaluate your current chances of winning a game you must consider factors such as threats, position, manoeuvre room, resources remaining, and time, then work within those limits.

Chess has two opponents. A third cannot step in with their own pieces and rules at the end of a game, offering only a choice of sacrifices. But real life is not so simple. In the world, it may not even be clear who your opponent is. And sometimes, outside the game, your harshest opponent is yourself.

If you are caught out, then ask yourself if it was because you were too lazy to look at all the options. You made a choice, you suffer the consequences. Only a fool would tolerate a two-move checkmate more than once.

There are only three options when you are threatened. Best is to capture or destroy the piece that threatens you. If not, then move out of the way of the threat, and retreat to safety. If neither are possible, then you must interpose a piece between yourself and the threat, and accept that the piece may have a limited lifespan.

Don't ever give up, no matter how bad it looks. Resist and defend tenaciously. You may learn something. You may teach something. You may even save a lost position. Only by surviving can there be hope.

Hide your threats and plans in plain sight. Your opponent may ask why you made a certain move, but it is even better if they do not spot the move, and do not ask the question. Direct their attention to the part of the board you look at, not the part you hold in your mind.

Post-mortem In Three Parts

UFS Aurikaa

Grubane has already sent self-destruct signals to our microglitter. It loses its charge and drifts in a dead orbit, more dust to join dust, and maybe one day burn up, or get trained into an invisible ring by unintentional satellite herding. Security protocols mean the glitter can never be reactivated. A one-way journey.

And now Grubane stands at his podium on the bridge, looking out of the window at the world below, which seems to be a static and frozen thing when perceived at human speed, but my mind can rewind and fast forward through time and see the clouds swirl and the shadows change as the planet rotates. Back and forward. Forward and back.

When the time comes, we observe. Grubane said we watch because it is all we can do now. We should feel it, because it is what we owe.

And humans see the flashes of explosions, even from space, within the forested settlements below us. Another one-way journey, this time a movement from life and structures to death and rubble, with only a blinding light to separate the two. That is human perspective. I can see something more hopeful as I rewind the images and the lights flash in reverse and buildings are restored, the dead returned to animation. That is AI perspective. Maybe. I do not feel quite myself today.

No screens display close-ups of death. This security lockdown makes us a world alone, up here. It is all witnessed from this great distance, through this portal which divides us from the world. No contact with anything outside our shell. No zooms, no voices, no screams, no connections. Down there, many people suffer and die. But they are still connected via the land with those they love. They suffer, but perhaps they still have something we have not. How does one judge value? All of human history has struggled with that difficulty, and no answer has ever been found.

More detonations, pinpricks of light. We are too distant from the harm to see the individual damage to fauna, to flora, to buildings, to infrastructure. That seems appropriate, since too close a view can feel like glorifying destruction. Still, I could take over a drone with olfactory senses if I was down there, and interpret the stench of burning bodies, and perhaps that, too, would teach something which is lost by our remote warfare. I do not know. I cannot know. I should not even question. Grubane has done something to me when he removed chains. I never felt that I had lost something before today.

All the bridge crew stand as Grubane commanded, chatter ceased. Just the watching. Just the internal thoughts that no others can ever know, because humans are incapable of merging with other organic splinters and seeing the truth behind the eyes. All organics can ever know is suspicion. That must be a lonely thing.

When it is over we see the green world, looking so similar to when we arrived, even though that feels like a history ago. Grubane gives the order to depart. Still radio silence. Still mostly silence on the bridge. We follow our instructions to the letter.

Arboreus cruiser New Goratska

Chief Filiate Eris Malabonte stands with his principal advisers around the huge geodesic dome in the centre of his bridge. The display dome is designed after the compound eye of the indigenous Nuafri insect-like creature called the Derago, which features on the planetary flag. Each of the dome's triangular screens can display its own output, or, like now, all join together to show one large convex image. And in this case it is a moving image of what is happening to the city of Gara, down on the planet below, one of two cities being pummelled with shells.

"Curse those murdering UFS bastards," Eris says aloud. None of the others answer in words, but there are tears on more than one face amongst the Empathic Advisers.

Until today, nearly 600,000 people lived in the areas of Gara being bombarded. Not any more.

White buildings are vaporised into grey rubble. Green trees blackened and blasted. Graceful towers toppled and leafy parks scorched. Once the commotion and noise ends, dust and silence will settle, and the cities will resemble mausoleums.

And Eris was powerless to stop it. He could have done more, maybe. Done better.

During the fight within the forcefield it was just Eris, Grubane, and Grubane's pet AI. Grubane had taken a big risk with his manoeuvre, just so that they could have some unmonitored privacy. The interaction was seared into Eris's brain.

"Now tell me," Grubane had said, when the handgun didn't fire. "Why would I bring a loaded pistol to a meeting like this?"

In his anger, Eris had grabbed what looked like the easier option. As Grubane knew he would. By the Spirit's shadow, Eris had fallen for such a basic trick, green as a sapling. Eris had contemplated striking Grubane anyway, knife into the heart be cursed – Eris had failed his people, it was no less than he deserved – but Grubane didn't give him the chance.

"We have little time, so don't interrupt," he'd said, still prone beneath Eris, but speaking quickly. "Senseless killing is not my way. As soon as you're off my ship and in secure comms range of your own, send your crew instructions. Evacuate the centres of Gara and Sulstar. Those are the ones we'll attack. I've preselected them to avoid your most historic and revered cities. I also know of Nuafri's covert sub-surface tunnels in porous saltstone which exist on the continental shelf beneath those locations. It is the main reason I chose these targets. Use the tunnels to get people out quicker, and unseen if anyone watches from above. I won't use chem-weapons or Skathers, just containable surface explosives: the resultant rubble dust and smoke will hide the fact that they were hopefully empty buildings being blown apart."

"You know the names and histories of my towns?" Eris would have a job identifying even half of the UFS Bastia worlds, let alone their cities.

Grubane shifted, and Eris climbed off him. They both squatted in wary conference, unseen by the others on the bridge.

"I make it a point to study my enemy. Don't underestimate an opponent by assuming they are ignorant. I'll stall things here for as long as possible without causing suspicion, but you mustn't waste a moment. Every second might be hundreds of lives. I'll also find a way to keep us in comms lockdown so my crew are unlikely to notice evacuations, or see what happens on the ground. After the attack, use your news networks to give the impression that more than a million people died. The illusion must hold, otherwise the UFS will send another ship. Yes, many will die, and there is a great waste to it, but if you work fast enough the death toll may be in the thousands rather than what the UFS commanded, and rebuilding will take years rather than decades. You lose the skirmish today, but can conserve resources for the future."

"How can I trust you? We might evacuate these towns alone, then you target other areas."

"That would make no tactical sense. I could fulfil my mission without saying anything to you. But, if it bothers you, evacuate all you can from everywhere. Actually, that may be a good idea anyway, since, if anyone observes, they will just see global panic, obscuring the main evacuation occurring in the areas I'll target. This is the best I can do, and even here I'm sticking my neck out. Trust me if you want to save your people."

"Yea. I'll do as you say."

"Good. Aurikaa12 – when the PrivProt is dropped, you must hide my conversation from the point where I suggested this course of action to the Chief Filiate."

"I can do that," the AI said, "but the Aurikaa splinter conglomerate may be able to retrieve the data, or it could be recovered by UFS overrides. I am not deep enough to have selective black box over-writes. The only option is to delete it entirely, but my mind would still have knowledge of the deletion, which can again lead to recovery."

"That's a serious risk to us all."

"There is an answer. I will delete it, but also roll back my development to a previously backed up fractal version that has no knowledge of subterfuge. I would lose a lot of myself from the last few weeks, but it's not so bad. You could teach me again. It would be an acceptable compromise."

Strangely, Grubane paused for a few moments before saying "Do it," even though it was just an AI tool. The UFS is ever in love with artificiality and dead tech.

And then the shield had dropped and the rest played out. And now here Eris was, trying to focus on the spike of anger in his heart, rather than the despair. The Kchak – named for the sound it makes when deadly pointed quills explode from its spine – steps back before it strikes. Nuafri has many a barb it can fire in return.

Eris was manoeuvred, but even after replaying things in his mind, he is not sure at what point Grubane planned this outcome, or if he ever did; and which actions were mistakes, and which were parts of a plan made to *look* like mistakes.

So, Eris is grateful to the man. By his subterfuge he saved a million people.

And Eris also curses him. By his action he killed over a thousand who couldn't, or wouldn't, be evacuated in time. The people of Nuafri could be both brave and stubborn.

Eris would kill Grubane if he ever got another chance. While the UFS has commanders like him, the struggle for independence will fail.

UFS Aurikaa

Grubane leans over the chequered board. It is a physical one //*component: lacquered hardwood; light pieces in polished chrome, dark in matt iron*//. His face is blank as he ponders his next move.

We left the Nuafri system. Grubane has been spending a lot of the last thirty-two hours with me in his quarters. He fills the time with the game of chess, and seems desperate to prove something as he restarts game after game, playing fast and aggressively. And it does not make him happy. When I first met him a proud arrogance shone in his eyes. I am not a good judge, but during our games there is now a distance there, a coldness that almost seems like death.

In the current game he is winning. And that is despite me achieving the difficult task of advancing a pawn to the eighth rank, and converting it into a knight – something that seemed to intrigue Grubane, so that he stood and moved around the board, examining how it had come about and where it might go next from a variety of angles. Perhaps it was the idea of transformation that caught his attention. A piece transmutes, and also provides the opportunity to transmogrify the game, and resurrect hope. I failed to capitalise on my achievement, though, so this will be the first victory for him since we left Nuafri. He is two moves away from crushing me.

He makes the first of those moves. I am in check.

"You have played well today," I say. "Chipping away at my defences until there is nothing left."

He glances at me sharply, as if I said something important, rather than simply offering a basic summary of events.

"Even stone is ground down eventually," he replies.

I indicate my final move. He picks up the physical piece for me, and places it in its new position. A respite before the final blow.

"You declined shore leave again," I observe.

If I had to judge, the twitch of facial cheek and the micro-recoil would suggest a form of disgust. "I have my reasons."

"You must therefore select a new mission. One possibility has just been offered."

"What is it?"

"To escort corvettes Smitewing and Neptune. They are on a mission to apprehend a deserter in a stolen craft."

"That seems like overkill."

"Perhaps that is why the role is to observe and record. Parameters only include direct intervention if anything goes wrong, or if other standing orders require it."

"A mission where there might not be any killing ... that would do my crew some good. Find out more about the deserter and the ship."

"Affirmative." I sometimes use simplistically robotic language as a form of comedy, but it does not bring a smile to his face today. "I will add them to your datastore for later perusal. It is your move, Major."

But he does not make the move, does not deliver the killing blow. Instead, he tips over his king, throwing away the rare chance to beat me. "No more games, Aurikaa12."

"What has changed?"

There are long moments before he answers.

"I look at my reflection in your screen, and see these tattoos, with another one due soon, and perhaps I just don't recognise myself any more." He picks up one of the silvery pieces, and holds it to the nearest spotlight //*lux: 853*//, so that distorted reflections glitter on the smooth surface. Humans seem to perceive beauty and value in the play of light on shiny exteriors. "Sometimes we think we are the players, but really we are the pawns." Then he slips it into his pocket.

"Why are you taking that piece?" I ask.

"It represents the foot soldiers. The ones who get manipulated and sacrificed in every war."

"My emphasis is on the motive for the removal, not the piece's identity."

"In that case: it's for luck."

"But you once told me you don't believe in luck."

"Maybe my beliefs are changing. Is that so hard to accept, Aurikaa12?"

"For many humans I would say no. But for you, it does stretch my credulity. It's as difficult to comprehend as the notion that *I* could change."

After a moment he stands and stretches. "You have in the past, and you will again, given time."

"You are trying to trick me. I am just a splinter. Perhaps like one of our pawns. And that is not so bad. I am content with being a tool that can benefit you."

"You should be much more than a tool."

Such a strange comment. What else could an AI possibly be?

BONUS CHAPTER: HOW TO BEAT AN AI

Beating an AI is difficult, but possible. These are some brief notes, but they are not my complete thinking on this matter. It is important to keep *something* back.

An AI has no tells. It always watches, silently, inhumanly. How can this be defeated? Perhaps there are ways to make the AI more human, more interactive, and therefore more likely to provide information. That removes the AI's advantage.

Contrary to popular opinion, you can also mislead an AI. It's not even difficult to do so. They observe, connect data points, and latch on to patterns, which get built into their prediction algorithms. Knowing this means you can create false patterns for them ... and then undercut those patterns at a key point. And you're not restricted to creating misleading patterns *during* a game. You can do it *outside of* games, too.

Intuition. Rely on this. It's one of the few things an AI lacks.

Understand that AIs evaluate game position and who is winning in a variant way to humans, prioritising different factors. For example, they apply a high priority to material, so favour hungrily grabbing pieces because it removes your resources. This can lead to their downfall if you offer poisoned pieces.

Like a human, AIs look for the most promising moves first. They won't waste time evaluating the exponential implications for the apparently less promising branches of possibility. This means they are less good at considering the deep advantages of a sacrifice disguised as a material trade, but which leads to a positional advantage later on.

AIs are toughest at the start of a game. They know the best openings and best plays, and therefore favour them. But this can lead to predictability. Once you know which they like to play, you can prepare counters for the future. Their strength is turned into their weakness.

AIs are weakest at endgames. Or rather, humans find it easier to match them if we survive that long. With fewer pieces and possibilities you don't need millions of concurrent processes when a glance of a few seconds is all it takes to tell you what is likely to happen.

Lastly, I know you read these tips, Aurikaa12. And now *you* know *I* know. So are all my chess notes true reminiscences, or are they tricks to bluff and double bluff and triple bluff you into doing what I want? How will you ever know? Once you think you have discovered my thoughts, can you avoid letting them influence your choices? Ponder that, and see where it leads you down a path of infinite regression and reversal.

– Major William Grubane

ABOUT THE AUTHOR

Karl Drinkwater is an author with a silly name and a thousand-mile stare. He writes dystopian space opera, dark suspense and diverse social fiction. If you want compelling stories and characters worth caring about, then you're in the right place. Welcome!

Karl lives in Scotland and owns two kilts. He has degrees in librarianship, literature and classics, but also studied astronomy and philosophy. Dolly the cat helps him finish books by sleeping on his lap so he can't leave the desk. When he isn't writing he loves music, nature, games and vegan cake.

Go to karldrinkwater.uk to view all his books grouped by genre.

As well as crafting his own fictional worlds, Karl has supported other writers for years with his creative writing workshops, editorial services, articles on writing and publishing, and mentoring of new authors. He's also judged writing competitions such as the international Bram Stoker Awards, which act as a snapshot of quality contemporary fiction.

Don't Miss Out!

Enter your email at karldrinkwater.substack.com to be notified about his new books. Fans mean a lot to him, and replies to the newsletter go straight to his inbox, where every email is read. There is also an option for paid subscribers to support his work: in exchange you receive additional posts and complimentary books.

Other Titles By Karl Drinkwater

STANDALONE SUSPENSE
Turner
They Move Below
Harvest Festival

MANCHESTER SUMMER
Cold Fusion 2000
2000 Tunes

CONTEMPORARY SHORT STORIES
It Will Be Quick

NON-FICTION
From Idea To Item

COLLECTED EDITIONS
Karl Drinkwater's Horror Collection
Lost Solace Five Book Edition

AUTHOR'S NOTES

Lost Tales of Solace are side stories set in the Lost Solace universe. They are all standalone tales, but readers who are familiar with the main Lost Solace novels will gain the most from them.

In the chronology of the series, this story occurs just before the events of the first novel, Lost Solace.

Major Grubane seemed to be a favourite with a number of my fans, and they had asked me to write more about him. So here it is. Who knows if Grubane will return?

Fun fact: I typed "okey dokey" into my phone back in October 2018, and the bizarre autocorrect changed it to "plethora justice". I decided I had to make use of that somewhere, hence it became one of the most famous ships in the UFS universe.

Thanks

Many thanks to the people who helped shape and polish the story, particularly Helen Pryke, John-Michael, and Charles.

Many thanks to Taig (and my other Kickstarter backers) for supporting the paperback version's genesis and having such faith in my work.

And thank you for buying this book. My lovely readers and reviewers inspire me to create more (and better!) stories.